The Star of Algiers

◆

Also by Aziz Chouaki

PUBLICATIONS

2003

Une Virée (play) Ed. Balland

2001

Avoir 20 ans à Alger, (fiction) Ed. Alternatives
Une Enfance Outremer, Le Seuil, points virgule (collective)
El Maestro, (play) Ed Théatrâles

2000

Aigle, (novel) Gallimard/Frontières

1998

Les Oranges, (contemporary tale) Ed. Mille et une Nuits

1989

Baya, (novel) Ed. Laphomic, Alger

1982

Argo, (poems, short stories) Ed. L'Unité, Alger

RADIO

Baya, play broadcast by France Culture (1992)
Fruits de mer, 24 short stories, Radio Suisse Romande (1993)
Brisants de mémoire, 5 plays, France Culture (1995)

THEATRE

Baya, directed by Michèle Sigal, Nanterre Amandiers, 1991

The Star of Algiers

A NOVEL

AZIZ CHOUAKI

Translated from the French by
Ros Schwartz and Lulu Norman

Graywolf Press
Saint Paul, Minnesota

First published in France by éditions Balland with the title *L'Étoile d'Alger*.
Copyright © éditions Balland 2002.
Translation copyright © 2005 by Ros Schwartz and Lulu Norman

Publication of this volume is made possible in part by a grant provided by the Minnesota State Arts Board, through an appropriation by the Minnesota State Legislature; a grant from the Wells Fargo Foundation Minnesota; and a grant from the National Endowment for the Arts, which believes that a great nation deserves great art. Significant support has also been provided by the Bush Foundation; Target and Mervyn's with support from the Target Foundation; the McKnight Foundation; and other generous contributions from foundations, corporations, and individuals. To these organizations and individuals we offer our heartfelt thanks.

MINNESOTA
STATE ARTS BOARD

NATIONAL
ENDOWMENT
FOR THE ARTS

A Lannan Translation Selection
Funding the translation and publication of exceptional literary works

Published by Graywolf Press
2402 University Avenue, Suite 203
Saint Paul, Minnesota 55114
All rights reserved.

www.graywolfpress.org

Published in the United States of America

ISBN 1-55597-412-0

2 4 6 8 9 7 5 3 1
First Graywolf Printing, 2005

Library of Congress Control Number: 2004104192

Cover design: Kyle G. Hunter

Cover photograph: © Simon Rowe/Photonica

FOR YASMINE

Contents

Part One

◆

One

Dark and spreading, a veil obscures the face of the sky, a grim mask covering the sun's eyes. Algiers's finery is blotted out. Bilious swollen clouds, ochre drizzle, earthquake weather.

The horizon's blotted out, too.

Cité Mer et Soleil, Djelloul's car pulls up in front of Block C, Moussa gets out, yawning. He bangs the door, bangs it again, and they part with a wave. The chorus . . . two or three times?

Check it later, argued with the bass player over it.

Bet you it's three times.

Pools of filth in front of the entrance. Moussa hitches up his trousers, hops nimbly between the puddles. Whoops . . . slips. Squelch. Splatters his beautiful, shiny 750-dinar shoes. Cursing, he takes out a little white handkerchief, spits on it, and wipes them clean.

The lobby of the apartment building is a war zone, letterboxes spewing their guts, walls and staircases crumbling. Kids, kids, and more kids.

A child of three, barefoot and naked to the waist, is splashing around in the murky water, his face tattooed with mud. He's playing with a dead bird, pulling out its feathers one by one.

Moussa looks away, steps over him, and makes for the staircase, dog-tired. Swarms of snot-nosed brats cluster in the stairwells.

The building's waking up, sullen faces, dry coughs, some to their sorrow, others keeping close to the walls. Schoolkids, workers, or young layabouts by decree of the Almighty.

In the street, cars refuse to start. Go on, put it in second, we'll push . . . one, two, three puuush . . . arms abound, thousands of strong sleepy arms. Push, push . . . is it the spark plugs? The battery? I know someone in Bouzaréah, might get you a battery if you're lucky.

A powerful stink of perfume corrupts the stale morning air. Hey, it's Wahiba, the Méziani girl. Divine ass . . . Hi, hi . . . secretary in a travel agency, I think.

Wonder what's going down at home?

It's Wednesday, so Saliha, Kahina, and Mohand must have left for work, Nacéra and Ouardia for college. The old man'll be devouring the politics section of the paper, railing against the government as usual.

Ma taking pills for her sciatica, her blood pressure, and her diabetes. Grandma already rolling the couscous, Z'hor doing the washing, the housework. Her girls, Maya and Fella, four and five, playing on the balcony. Sahnoun, unemployed idiot, autistic for years, will still be sleeping. And Slimane, unemployed Islamist, he's bound to be at the mosque with the bearded brigade.

Entrance 9, staircase F, 5th floor, the landing, apartment 35. Wiped out, Moussa fumbles for his key and softly opens the door, dreading the reception he'll get.

Splitting headache. What a night!

All in all, the gig went well, well organized, well paid at any rate, 20,000 dinars in total, 8,000 for yours truly. That's only right: I'm the star. It's no joke, singing for over five hours with just one short break. Typical wedding repertoire: a bit of traditional Algiers for starters, to relax them, then you go straight for the gut, the *pièce de résistance,* a modern Kabyle song, chef's specialty. There was even a journalist from *Algérie Actualité,* big mustache . . . arranged to meet . . . an interview maybe?

Has to be said, I gave it my all, everyone danced till first light. The violinist went a bit off-key, but it was OK. Then we partied with the band at the Terminus until dawn, thirty-six coffees, sandwiches. The usual early-morning customers, musicians, cabaret dancers. Then, around 7 a.m., back home with Djelloul, our band driver.

I make a point of coming home in the early hours. It's better like that, you crash out instantly, don't see so much.

Fourteen people in three rooms.

As I open the door, a quick peek, Fella rushes up and gives me a big hug, I slip her a 10-dinar coin, tiptoe along the corridor, and dive into the boys' bedroom.

Sahnoun's still sleeping, Slimane's already out and about. Fumbling, Moussa undresses then flops onto his mattress on the floor and sinks into sleep.

◆

Torrid awakening around 4 p.m., kids yelling, women shrieking and arguing on the landing, radios blaring at full volume, cars hooting, drafts, doors slamming.

Something pressing on his forehead, it's Maya's little mitt, her cool muzzle kissing him. A breath of life, Moussa cuddles the little girl and is cradled by the tinkle of her laughter.

Sahnoun's sitting on his mattress, his back against the wall and his nose in a detective novel. They're all he reads, hasn't left the room for over ten years, except when he's taken to the hospital for tests. Totally autistic, Sahnoun talks only to himself, using few words. He's forty-eight.

Moussa gets up, does a few exercises, then, tripping over Maya, he rummages in his jacket pockets and brings out a pack of Marlboros, which he hands to his big brother. Sahnoun's daily pleasures: cigarettes and detective novels. His eyes shine with gratitude.

Bathroom, quick wash, no water. Moussa takes some from the jerrican and gives his face a cat-lick in front of the mirror: good-looking guy, got to admit it. See the dentist about that tooth. Smile's got to be dazzling, that's how you get to be Michael Jackson.

In the kitchen, Ma's already clattering her pots and pans, moaning and groaning, rheumatism, diabetes. Quick kiss on the forehead, she pours me a coffee that I drink on the hoof.

From where I stand, I can see the frame with the photo of Mouloud on top of the TV. Family hero, died fighting for the resistance, gun in hand. It was war, Independence.

Every time Ma does the cleaning, she wipes the photo and sheds a tear.

In the living room, Pa scans the papers listening to the radio, a surly grunt for a greeting. Hasn't spoken to me for years, since I spelled out my career to him, looking him straight in the eyes: professional singer. Violent arguments. Since then, heavy silence on both sides.

He took it as a betrayal, he wanted me to be a departmental manager or something like that.

Back to the kitchen. I hand Ma a bundle of notes, a quarter of yesterday's pay. As always, she takes it, protesting.

Z'hor, my big sister, walks through the kitchen carrying a huge basin of water. Water's been turned off.

In the corridor, Fella's carefully decapitating her doll. Drafts, windows bang, Pa yells from the living room. Feel very, very groggy.

On the balcony, Grandma and Z'hor are spreading out the couscous to dry. Stumble over Maya and Fella and go back to my room.

Sahnoun's deep in his SAS novel, cigarette in mouth. With a heavy heart, I put on my USA tracksuit and pick up my mandola. Then I go down the stairs, keeping a low profile and steering clear of the gangs of kids.

Practice the latest hit from the charts. Moussa heads for the patch of wasteland behind the apartment building, looking out over the sea, the great Bay of Algiers.

Mer et Soleil housing project, brutal buildings mired in mountains of refuse, nobody gives a damn in this country. Well, I couldn't give a damn either, I'm going to leave this shit hole and be a big star. Paris, London, New York, showbiz . . .

Sky's still black.

Garbage bins spilling their innards, overflowing with junk, burnt-out domestic appliances, old tires . . . Moussa finds himself a little corner.

Free at last, this is the place he loves to work. At home it's impossible, no space. He sits looking out to sea, garbage bins behind him.

His pride and joy, a Walkman, 3,000 dinars on the black market, a good deal. He rolls a fat joint and starts work, learning the latest hit by Takfarinas, the megastar of modern Kabyle music.

Moussa knows he can show Takfarinas a thing or two, it's just a question of time. He's aiming for the stars, he is. Yeah, Michael Jackson, Prince, the USA, far from the Arabs, far from frizzy-haired poverty and shit brown skin . . .

Earphones clamped to his head, he sings at the top of his voice. Rewinds, gets the rhythm of the chorus, counting the beats, pulls on his joint and begins again, singing his head off.

Hey, what did I say? It is three times for the chorus. Get them to listen to the cassette, shove it up that bassist's . . .

Moussa goes back to the beginning, even more enthusiastically. He snaps a string on his mandola, oh shit . . . fix the string, a tight knot'll do it, at least for today. But got to get another set of strings soon.

He carries on singing, tapping his foot as hard as he

can. Gray sea before him, the waste ground, garbage, the kids playing in it are laughing.

They all know Moussa Massy. Been on the radio twice, and a quarter of a column in the paper, page 16, the rising star of modern Kabyle music.

Why Moussa Massy?

It's my stage name. In fact, my name's Méziane Boudjiri, but you obviously won't get anywhere with a name like that. It was Rachid who thought of it. Massy's short for Massinissa, Berber king, third century BC. Or was it the eighth century? Must check. And Moussa because it sounds good, Moussa Massy, Mss Mss, M. and M., yeah, it sounds good. In a few years, when I'm famous, it'll be just Massy on its own.

Moussa writes his name everywhere: Massy, on his jeans, on tablecloths, on the walls of the john in bars, on his mandola, everywhere, Moussa Massy, Moussa Massy.

The cassette slows down, the batteries, shit, no more batteries anywhere, maybe on the black market, ten times the price. Moussa doesn't care, he'll buy whatever he needs, at any price. You have to aim high, reach for the sky: Michael Jackson.

It's thanks to Rachid that Moussa's career's taking off. Seeing him later anyway, maybe he'll have a copy of the poster?

He ripples with pleasure at the thought: a poster of him, with Moussa Massy in big letters, purple on a yellow background. He trusts Rachid's talent—he's a graphic designer, a real artist.

Moussa takes off the headphones and sings the number again, yelling. Crystal clear notes, scales, juicy chunks of song with operatic vibrato, Andalusian, flamenco, Julio Iglésias . . .

Oh shit, I'd kill to do my own cassette, my own tracks! Every idiot has already put out a cassette, there's no reason . . .

Around 5 p.m., he goes back up to the apartment, keeping his head down. The bearded kamis-wearers are everywhere, beards, kamis, beards, kamis.

He does his best to hide his mandola, he knows what they must be saying: clown, Satan's henchman, faggot, etc.

Moussa climbs the stairs, gritting his teeth, trips over a kid blocking his way. With a violent kick, he sends him flying.

"Get the fuck out of my way!"

The brat swears back and throws stones at him. Moussa puts his mandola down and chases him, pissed as hell. He disappears among the garbage bins, other kids laugh and cheer. Finally Moussa pins him against a lamppost, holding him by the throat.

Breathless, he snarls in his ear:

"Listen up, any more shit from you and I'll have your ass. Get it?"

Some adults step in, mostly Islamists, preaching peace, for God is the only Judge, blah, blah, blah . . .

Moussa swallows his anger, apologizes, picks up his mandola, and goes up to his apartment watched by the gleeful crowd. Free entertainment.

Seeks sanctuary in his room.

Sahnoun, impassive, is still absorbed in his SAS. He's a big 48-year-old kid, inner bliss. Sahnoun's right, happiness is silence.

Slimane's there too, wispy goatee, gray kamis, reading religious books, pages yellow from use.

Wordlessly, Moussa puts down his mandola and stretches out on the mattress. Calm, yoga, calm.

Above his bed is a small shelf collapsing under the piles of cassettes, old magazines, *L'Express, VSD, Paris-Match*, a Michael Jackson poster. Little mementos, postcards, Paris, London, a Spanish doll, African bracelet, shades, address book. A few books: *Berber Tales and Legends* by Isabelle Rakowski, a biography of Pelé by Edmund Jaspers, *The Truth about the Assassination of Kennedy* by Jack W. Rafferty, volume two of *War and Peace*, which he's never opened, an old Larousse with half the letter A amputated, a copy of the National Charter, two *Robinson Crusoes*, God knows why, and *The Repudiation* by Rachid Boudjedra, which he's never understood.

Moussa gets his head together. Hang in there . . . he knows that only music . . . hang in there, they don't get it, maybe one day . . . When they see me on TV, on satellite, yeah, Moussa Massy in concert at Bercy, or in New York. That'll be the day, yeah, but it'll be too late for them, they can go fuck themselves, the lot of them. He'll show them.

Yeah, that's it, show the whole lot of them.

Slimane comes over to him timidly, stroking his beard: "Méziane, you couldn't . . . I . . . my shoes are ripped, they're the only ones I've got. You . . . just 200 dinars, God will . . ."

Moussa, mad:

"Can't give you 200 dinars at the mosque, huh? The god squad can only criticize, it's all sin, sin. My dough's the devil's money, it comes from music, it's sin, you know that, don't you?"

Slimane lowers his eyes. Moussa's his big brother, respect.

Moussa looks at him. Slimane's buggered, his soul's already in the jaws of God, the yelling bearded guy—God, I mean.

Slimane used to be so adorable, gentle and innocent, a fresh young stripling . . . I can picture him not so long ago imitating George Michael, blushing, trying to chat up the girl on the third floor. What the hell happened?

Slimane's about to leave, but Moussa grabs him:

"Wait, moron, here's your 200 dinars. Find yourself a job, be a man, stop hanging out with the beards! Oh, who cares, do what you like, it's not my problem. Everyone can sort out their own shit."

Muttering his thanks, Slimane pockets the note, his eyes downcast. Caressing his pack of Marlboros, Sahnoun hasn't looked up from his SAS.

Sahnoun's built up a whole local network without ever leaving his bedroom—a dozen SAS addicts who swap thrillers. About once a week they come to the apartment for a brief, wordless exchange, especially Djelloul, the local mechanic. Gone on like that for years.

Lying on his mattress, Moussa breathes, glances sidelong at Michael Jackson's smile on the wall; it makes him brave.

And then there's the journo from yesterday, could mean an interview. Oh if only . . . talk to Rachid about it.

Nearly 6 p.m., see Rachid, yeah, does me good. He's the only one who understands. Moussa loves talking to Rachid, it's always productive, he's so clever, always lifts his spirits.

Change his look. He takes off his tracksuit, puts on a pair of jeans, moccasins, a Benetton T-shirt, and a black Danton jacket: perfect. In the corridor, he runs into Ouardia and Nacéra, back from college, affectionate kisses, his little sisters look up to him.

Moussa slips them a 100-dinar note.

"You'll have to cut it in half," he says, leaving them in fits of giggles.

The apartment's beginning to fill up, fourteen people in three rooms. Only Mohand's not home yet, back from work around 7:00, warehouseman at Sonatmag. And Kahina, checkout girl at the Pins Maritimes supermarket, back around 7:00, too.

Saliha's already there, high-school math teacher in Kouba. Apple of their eye—math teacher, no wonder. Saliha's just turned thirty-four, not married yet.

She waylays Moussa:

"Hey, when are you going to bring back the water pump? The engine's about to pack up. You said today! I don't give a shit, Méziane, if the car dies, it's your problem. I've had it, I'm the one who pays the insurance and everything . . ."

Abashed, annoyed, Moussa:

"OK, OK. I'm going to see a guy tonight. Don't worry, I'll get your pump." The Ritmo had become part of the family. Saliha paid twelve million for it last year, a steal. It was made in 1980, exactly ten years ago.

Moussa doesn't have a driver's license, keeps saying next month.

Fourteen people in three rooms, living on four salaries plus the old man's pension, a pittance every three months. Too many people, yeah.

And Mohand, who's forty-five. He's supposed to be getting married next year. He's already put it off three years, nowhere to live, even though he's got a good job . . .

They're all starting to bawl, the kids, Pa and his ulcer, Z'hor and Ma at the stove, the space is shrinking. Moussa's suffocating. Time to go out, get some air, see Rachid.

Saliha managed to get hold of some Zantak for Pa's ulcer, 500 dinars on the black market, that might calm him down a bit.

Thirty years' service as a bus conductor, you don't get out unscathed. The Parade Ground to Ben Aknoun, the longest route, crammed with people, wheezing up the Colonne Voirol, catching the fare-dodgers, threatening them with the big stick if necessary. Pa retired eight years ago.

A pungent smell of couscous fills the apartment, Z'hor's just removed the lid. They're all waiting for Kahina so they can sit down to dinner. She's supposed to be sneaking some Gruyère home from the supermarket, there was a delivery this week. The girls are already talking about making potato gratin tomorrow. Ouardia reminds everyone of the first time Grandma saw Gruyère and thought it was soap.

Giggles erupt from the kitchen, followed by the helpless laughter of the two girls.

A loud roar answers from the living room. It's Pa demanding absolute silence, he's reading *Horizons*, the evening paper.

That sends Moussa heading for the door.

Whew, he's outside, clusters of kamis-wearing beards around the garbage bins and puddles of piss.

A passing greeting, Moussa notices some new beards. Look, even Spartacus, I don't believe it . . .

A sad little creep, hardened alcoholic, partial to *zombretto*.

And Baiza, too, the bus-stop mugger. Moussa saw him open a guy up last year. One slash of the razor and whoosh, the guy's guts fell into his hand.

Well, well, isn't Islam a fine thing!

The clusters of beards freeze, voices tail off. All of a sudden, they crane their necks, their lust-filled gazes converge. It's Wahiba, the Méziani girl, coming home from work in a mini-dress, radiant with desire.

A pack of brats, average age ten, wolf whistle as she passes. Some whip out their cocks and wave them around, yelling:

"Hey, Wahiba, give us a fuck!"

"Don't you want to come and suck me, Wahiba?"

"Oh, look at how she wiggles that ass . . . mmm, I'd like to screw that!"

Superb in her dignity, Wahiba ignores them, sashaying provocatively. She knows she drives them crazy, she loves it. Flicking back a strand of hair, she darts Moussa a smile, and he returns it just as covertly.

Yeah, fuck it, corner her under a staircase . . . oh, just give her a good, quick fuck, nothing more. His heart's already spoken for: Fatiha, the sweet and innocent light of his life, is due back from her grandfather's funeral in Kabylia on Friday.

A mule cart: a fruit and vegetable man stations himself outside the building and sells tomatoes, 50 dinars a kilo. Baskets are lowered on ropes from balconies.

A cab draws up, Moussa jumps in, heads for Cité Garidi, a new housing development, all executives and intellectuals.

The taxi's like a mobile mosque, smell of musk, FIS stickers, Allah, verses of the Koran, taped sermons by the virulent Ali Benhadj blasting from the speakers.

Shades, chewing gum, bit of a paunch, the driver curses the women not wearing the hijab, whores all of them. But it'll all change soon, the FIS'll soon clean things up, you'll see.

Moussa nods in feigned agreement, change the strings on the mandola, get hold of a water pump. The cab takes the Ben Aknoun turnoff.

◆

Cité Garidi, the cab pulls up outside apartment building A, Moussa pays and steps out. Immaculate neighborhood, this could be Switzerland—green manicured lawns, car parks, a far cry from Cité Mer et Soleil.

Women pushing prams stand chatting on the sidewalk, they're not wearing hijabs. Not many kids. Anyhow, they're not the same here—fair-haired, neat and tidy, they look like they're Swedish.

Second floor, new-age chimes, Rachid opens the door. He's wearing baggy black pants and a white T-shirt, there's jazz playing. He ushers Moussa in.

Rachid's father's a diplomat in London, gave this big three-room apartment to his son who lives in it alone—yeah, alone! Rachid started up his ad agency last year. It's doing well, he's got clients, works hard.

The apartment's spacious, light, pictures painted by Rachid, little green spotlights. In a corner, an acoustic guitar, tumba drums, a powerful hi-fi system, CD player, one of the first in Algiers.

Rachid and I met doing our national service in the Navy. We were based in La Pérouse, an idyllic little port. I was an NCO. Rachid turned up eight months later. He was under me, then he became sub-lieutenant. The good years.

Rachid turns down the music:

"How'd it go last night?"

Moussa, taking off his jacket:

"Good, the usual wedding thing, till eight o'clock in the morning."

Rachid opens the fridge:

"What are you drinking? Heineken? Carlsberg? Whiskey?"

Moussa, hands on his knees:

"Whatever you're having, go on, set 'em up!"

Rachid takes out glasses, ice:

"I'm on the vodka. Vodka orange?"

"Suits me."

They clink glasses. Moussa just can't get over Rachid's place, it's incredible, you could be in Paris or New York, it must always be like that, *over there.*

Rachid leaves the sitting room and comes back with a big folder of drawings:

"Here, I've got a proof of the poster. Take a look, it's not bad."

He opens the huge portfolio and takes out an A3 poster. Moussa's speechless: Is that him? Hair greased back, '50s look, black-and-white tinted, just a splash of color, yellow sepia background with Moussa Massy written in round purple letters.

Moussa drools with delight. It hasn't quite sunk in yet, hard to believe it's him. Rachid inspects the poster, looking at it from the side:

"They haven't got the background quite right, I wanted more tone gradation, a tiny touch of yellow. I think they've overdone it a bit, but on the whole it's OK, isn't it?"

Moussa devours the poster with his eyes:

"Er . . . yes, it's . . . brilliant . . . well, I think so, anyway."

Rachid:

"Good, well that's perfect. I'll keep this one, touch it up a bit. Tomorrow I'll get it to the printer and we can roll some off. Five hundred to start with, and then we'll see, OK?"

Draining his glass, Moussa:

"Yeah, that's cool, and . . . when will they be ready?"

Rachid, pouring two more vodka oranges:

"In around two weeks. I know the printer, I'll keep an eye on things. Don't worry, he'll do a good job."

Moussa, rubbing his hands:

"Oh, I trust you. I'm in your hands."

Rachid puts down the poster, with a roguish grin:

"And . . . did you get hold of any . . . gear?"

Moussa takes out a brown stick of hash. Rachid's little weakness. Moussa supplies him—no sweat, everybody's dealing at Cité Mer et Soleil.

Rachid picks up the hash:

"Mmm. Shit that smells good. How much do I owe you?"

Moussa, laughing:

"Nothing . . . Respect, that's all."

Rachid, raising the hash to the skies:

"Well, respect to Massy, the new star of Kabyle song!"

The doorbell chimes, it's Farid and Sam, guitarist and drummer, friends of Rachid's, Moussa knows them, two cool customers.

Tall, with long hair, Farid sprawls in an armchair. Sam's already opened the fridge:

"Shit, Farid, there's Ayeneken, Kabyle beer, wow!"

Moussa's slightly subdued. Rachid plays Farid the latest Miles Davis, and an elastic sound fills the air.

Farid picks up the acoustic guitar and improvises on it, just like that, by ear, pure skill, Wes Montgomery. Sam sits down at the tumbas and accompanies him, light, subtle, perfectly in tune.

Staggered by their skill, Moussa tries to memorize it, the fingerwork, the rhythm. It's too fast for him, too sophisticated, but he wants to get it. That's exactly what he wants.

When the record ends, Farid sings some George Benson, Sam does the chorus, Moussa drinks in their pure brilliance.

Finale, Farid puts down the guitar and takes the joint from Rachid:

"Amazing, Farid, really bluesy voice, still into Ray Charles, aren't you?"

Farid, blowing out the smoke:

"For me, he's the daddy."

Stocky and strong, Sam breaks into "Georgia on My Mind," with a Kabyle accent, winking at Moussa.

Moussa hoots with laughter, raises his glass in appreciation. Rachid switches on the video, it's Prince. Moussa laps it all up, of course, that's it . . . Prince . . . that's exactly what he needs. He clocks every gesture, every glance, what they're wearing, the whole performance.

A bit later, Farid and Sam get to their feet, playing at Le Triangle, Algiers's hottest nightclub.

Rachid promises to drop in around 2 a.m., he's got to

pick up Lynd', his girlfriend, she's gone to a reception at the Bensidhoums.

Once they're alone again, Moussa tells him about the journalist yesterday, meeting next week, could mean an article.

Rachid's face lights up:

"Cool! We have to prepare the ground, plan your answers, professional, right. Oh yeah, that's great news. Who is this journalist?"

Moussa finishes rolling a joint, runs his tongue along the gummed edge of the paper:

"His name's Kamel Hamidi. Oh shit! It's got to happen. Touch wood."

Rachid knows everyone in Algiers, the artists, the intellectuals:

"Yeah, I know him, he's the culture editor at *Algérie Actualité*. Well, let's hope he won't be too smarmy. Whatever. We'll plan it properly. You can't just say anything, an article can stick to your ass for the rest of your life."

They celebrate. Rachid pours more drinks and starts briefing Moussa on his career—image, media, producers, style, contracts. Moussa gets it, doesn't want to stay a nobody, no, Moussa wants to become MASSY, the new star of modern Kabyle music.

Around 10 p.m., Moussa gets to his feet, got to go and meet Derdiche about the water pump. Rachid gives him a lift in his brand-new Fiat Uno, shag carpeting, powerful car radio purring.

Two

Derdiche lives in Belcourt, at the end of a blind alley, ugly neo-grunge architecture, breeze blocks, corrugated iron. Six families live in the building, including Derdiche's.

Moussa met him at a party in Beau Fraisier. Derdiche was drunk, he promised Moussa he'd find him a water pump. The entire family's been trying to get hold of one for two months, there wasn't one to be had anywhere, not even on the black market. Derdiche is their last hope.

Moussa ducks into an alleyway behind the Roxy cinema, veers left, and comes out at the dead end where Derdiche lives, two alleyways farther on.

Three long whistles. Nothing. Moussa whistles again and a shadow emerges from the shadows:

"Who is it? What d'you want?"

Moussa, folding his arms:

"Oh . . . Sorry, I . . . I'm looking for Derdiche."

The shadow:

"He's not here, he's at the Roxy."

The sky scintillates with stars, Moussa heads back toward the Roxy, it's ages since he's been to the movies. Outside the door, hordes of brats selling anything and everything on little makeshift tables: peanuts, cigarettes, batteries, medicines, firecrackers. Moussa buys a packet of Marlboros, 80 dinars.

Revenge of the Dragon is showing.

Their eyes rimmed with kohl, long henna-stained beards, Islamists in Afghan robes are selling religious magazines, worry beads, musk, religious objects, and holy water from Mecca.

Moussa goes up to the ticket seller, mint tea, soccer match on the crackling radio, and spins him some story, going to see a friend, family business, just a couple of minutes, I'll leave you my ID card. The guy says OK and lets him in.

In the theater, harsh lights, one hell of a din. The image is jumping on the screen, faded, saturated colors, interference on the sound track, copy of a copy of a copy of a copy.

Voices call down from the balcony to the stalls, frenzied whistles whenever any part of a woman appears on screen. Go for it, screw her, for fuck's sake!

A guy in slippers and pajamas is standing up, holding a basket. Come to fish out his kids and march them home, thwacking them with a sandal all the way.

In a corner, a gang of kids sit eating oranges around a huge ghetto-blaster pumping out loud reggae. They pelt the guys on the balcony with the rinds.

Limping on his crutch, a sandwich seller hawks *merguez*, doughnuts, soda.

From time to time, some kind of bouncer makes a

vigorous intervention with a big stick, no pissing in the theater, please!

Guys on the balcony throw firecrackers at the guys in the stalls. Moussa scans the faces, trying to pick out Derdiche. A bottle of soda whizzes past his ear and smashes into the screen, hoots of laughter all around. Brandishing his stick, the bouncer charges in again, threatening them.

At last Moussa spots Derdiche right at the back of the theater, he's with friends . . . Roast chicken, *harissa,* olives, bottles of wine. Derdiche waves enthusiastically, inviting him to join them.

Proudly, Derdiche introduces Moussa to his friends, famous modern singer. Moussa acts modest, wonders how he can be quick, get Derdiche on his own, sort out the water pump, get out of this hellhole.

But it's tricky, Derdiche is in an advanced state of drunkenness. He stands up, slips on something and falls at Moussa's feet. Lying on his back like a cockroach, he waves his arms, helpless with laughter. Moussa holds out a hand and helps him up. Once on his feet, Derdiche tells him that the water pump is at his friend Gabès's house, a couple of minutes away.

Phew, the water pump's there, that's the main thing.

Accompanied by a skinny youth, Derdiche and Moussa leave the Roxy, cross the main boulevard, and head toward the Kabul mosque. At least two hundred beards are outside, sitting on the tarmac, stopping the traffic, Allah is great.

Deafening bullhorn, the imam's trembling voice announces the imminence of the Last Judgment. Full of venom, the voice grows ever more hysterical, proclaiming the Jihad, to put an end, once and for all, to the infidel powers, and to all Communists, pork-eating unbelievers, women, hypocrites, and all those who aren't *proper* Muslims.

Moussa feels sick, his pulse races.

Weaving his way through the crowd of worshippers, Moussa feels someone tug the hem of his jacket, and turns around. I don't believe it, it's Yacine, the drummer from the band Mitidja! Don't tell me he's an Islamist, too?

Yacine, playboy of La Madrague beach, red-wine-and-prawn champion, the best bebop dancer in Tipaza, the only one who's screwed Mimi the hairdresser.

Moussa knows Yacine well, his family of twelve lives in two rooms, he hasn't worked since he broke his arm, he's way past thirty-eight . . .

In fact, Moussa does understand: Yacine grew *tired.*

In fact, that's how you end up an Islamist, it's when you get *tired. Tired* of dreaming, loving, living. That's how they'd got some of his best buddies. When you're so *tired,* you can't see them coming anymore.

Vague exchange of pleasantries, fine, yes and you, I'm good, and how's so-and-so. The conversation ends just as vaguely, see you around.

Moussa joins Derdiche and his skinny young crony, they walk up to the Belcourt heights, kids swarming everywhere, garbage, the smell of hash, piss, humid heat. Moussa thinks of Rachid and Cité Garidi . . .

Making their way through a maze of winding streets, the little group stops in front of a dilapidated shack. On the wall, written in huge, red dripping letters: TIRE REPAIRS.

Just below, in the same lettering, VICTORY TO THE FIS.

The garage is locked. A thin shaft of orange light filters through the holes in the iron shutter. Derdiche raps on the shutter, calling Gabès, he's the water-pump guy.

A tall, drooping figure sidles over to the doorway at the side. It's Gabès. He lets them in.

There are two guys there already, sandwiched between stacks of worn tires. On the ground, bottles of wine, eight empty and three full.

Moussa tries to squeeze himself between the tire iron and a tub of murky water.

Barefoot, pants rolled up, Gabès offers him a tractor tire:

"Sit there, Gabès, it's a real plush armchair. Sit down, handsome."

Gabès calls everyone Gabès, so everyone calls him Gabès.

Moussa willingly accepts the tire and the ritual sip of wine. He passes the bottle to Gabès, who wipes the neck on his tattered *Cambridge University* sweatshirt.

On the wall, old posters—Maradona, a 1982 calendar with a photo of a blonde in a swimsuit in a Porsche. The blonde's crotch has been mutilated with a screwdriver.

An acrid smell of tire rubber, inner-tube adhesive, and hash mingles with the stink of piss from the blocked toilet that has no door. Viscous heat, wan light, dying bulb dangling from a bare wire.

Moussa watches Gabès's grimy, cracked hands rolling a fat joint. He just wants to grab the water pump and get the hell out of there.

But he knows you can't do that. Hospitality, social codes.

After three joints, another bottle of wine and an idle conversation, Derdiche announces the reason for their visit.

Gabès stands up and wipes his hands on a rag that's black with grease:

"Oh hell yes, the water pump: it's a real steal! Is it for you, Gabès?"

Moussa nods, Gabès rummages in an old metal cupboard. His two friends haven't said a word yet, completely out of it, a fat bald guy and a short skinny one.

Lying on a bit of cardboard, the short skinny guy rolls onto his side and pisses into the tub of murky water.

Derdiche, off his head, is rolling a joint, fumbling for the skins, which are in front of him.

Gabès straightens up, closes the metal cupboard, which won't shut, and proudly holds up a brand-new water pump:

"You're lucky, Gabès, it's the last one, there won't be any more for six months. God is with you, Gabès! You must have been born under a lucky star!"

Gabès solemnly puts the water pump down in the center of the group. All eyes gaze at it, gleaming, haloed in light. The lanky youth picks it up and strokes it admiringly.

Moussa immediately asks how much he owes, and Gabès's expression turns apologetic:

"Oh, they have no fear of God, brother! The bastards upped the price. There's the guy's commission, grease everyone's palms, you know, and . . . I don't take a cut, oh no, no, you're a friend of Gabès, you're my brother. OK, let's say . . . 3,000 dinars, since you're my brother."

Moussa's stunned. That's at least fifteen times the price.

What price?

He rummages in his pockets and takes what's left of last night's pay, 4,000 dinars. He gives Gabès 3,000, which he accepts in God's name. Then brings out a bottle to celebrate. Derdiche wants to open it, he rummages around for the corkscrew.

Gabès turns to Moussa:

"You know, Gabès, if you need anything at all, come and see your brother Gabès. Anything you want, even . . . hold on, I want to show you something."

He ducks out of the workshop. Meanwhile, Derdiche has finally opened the bottle with a screwdriver. He takes a long slug and then passes it around.

Gabès comes back a moment later, holding a shining Kalashnikov.

Moussa's suddenly very scared. Everyone gazes at the gun in silence. The faces of the bald fat guy and the short skinny one are blank.

29

Gabès clicks the breech and aims at imaginary targets:

"This is a beast, brother! These days, you need a gun, gotta shoot all the faggots, the bastards, the rich scum, clean up the crap. The shit'll hit the fan soon and if you're not armed, you're fucked. Everyone's gonna pay, it's the Last Judgment . . . *Allah O Akbar!*"

His head resting on a pile of heavily patched old inner tubes, Derdiche:

"And how much do you want for it?"

Gabès aiming the gun at him:

"This? Oh, it's cheap . . . 20,000. Rocket launchers, grenades, revolvers, you name it, I'll get it. The brothers are watching, we're going to blow the whole fucking lot sky high! Yeah, man!"

Waving his Kalashnikov, Gabès starts to yell. Terrified, Moussa's convinced the cops'll burst in or something. Cold sweat, get the hell out, yeah, wait for the right moment, a *suitable* lull in the conversation, and make a run for it.

The wine's finished. A manic glint in his eye, Gabès suggests a *zombretto,* rubbing his hands together. He produces two bottles, ethanol and grenadine syrup. When he's mixed the two in an empty bottle, he shakes the whole thing vigorously. Satisfied, he takes a copious swig, belches out of the side of his mouth, then passes the bottle to Moussa. No way can he refuse.

First sip: his chest's on fire, his eyes, it tastes vile. Moussa feels like he's choking, wants to puke up his soul. Gabès is doubled up with laughter:

"Clears the tubes, eh Gabès?"

The bottle of *zombretto* passes from one to the other. The fat bald guy and the short skinny one take slugs without batting an eyelid. Derdiche sucks from the bottle, his eyes popping out of his head.

Conversation's begun to dry up, a dull fug of onomatopoeic grunts and groans, Gabès screeching an Andalusian lullaby.

Around midnight, there's a *suitable* lull in the conversation and Moussa makes the most of it. Apologizes, got to get home. Derdiche decides to sleep in the garage. Moussa thanks Gabès and Derdiche, says good-bye to everyone and walks out.

Once outside, he breathes in deep the balmy night air, the sweet smells of basil and barbecued meat. The French TV news signature tune can be heard coming from a house, satellite dish.

He can't get the Kalashnikov out of his mind.

Or the *zombretto*.

Every element of the Kalashnikov is in the *zombretto*.

Deeply unsettled, he walks down toward the little square in Belcourt, clutching the water pump. Take a cab, get back home.

As he walks, he adds up the figures, how fast cash gets eaten up . . . How much of last night's 8,000 dinars was left? A thousand? Crazy how it slips through your fingers! But it'll be OK, another wedding at the end of the month. And from June on, there'll be lots, at least three weddings a week. Yeah, it'll be OK. Buy a set of strings for the mandola, don't fuck up, got to get them before Thursday!

Feeling ravenous, haven't eaten today, completely lost track, nightlife. He comes to the main boulevard swarming with people. Despite the late hour, kids physically occupy the sidewalks, selling everything and anything. The air's very clammy, everything sticks to your skin.

Moussa spots a rickety snack kiosk to his right. He orders a cheese sandwich and a lemonade to get rid of the taste of *zombretto.*

A kitsch kiosk, pale colors, glaring light, totally Islamist esthetic. On the counter, a huge radio blares out verses of the Koran at full volume. The stick-thin waiter with a bushy beard, lost in his vast kamis, brings Moussa's order, and he pays at once.

Huddled near the cash register, Moussa sees a newspaper photo pinned to the wall: the leaders of the FIS, Abassi Madani and Ali Benhadj, with a caption in green felt tip: *In sh'Allah . . .*

It takes away his appetite, doesn't know where to look to eat in peace, dodgy cheese, the lemonade's worse, acid aftertaste.

He suddenly notices a fly buzzing around in his glass. Urge to vomit. He stops mid-chew and calls the waiter over, pointing at the fly. Unfazed, the waiter picks up a spoon and fishes out the fly. There you are, no problem. Moussa complains, and the waiter offers him another drink.

Moussa gives up and leaves the kiosk, gripping the water pump. Sickened, he opens his sandwich, chucks out the cheese and eats the bread halfheartedly. Stave off hunger.

Kids pounce on the cheese on the ground. Moussa stands on the curb. Cab, go home.

Fatiha, her big green eyes, her velvet smile . . . Moussa suddenly feels clean, the mere thought of her washes away all the shit surrounding him. To think it's five years now . . .

A chaste love, I swear. Moussa, a gentleman in this respect, not before marriage, no problem. But to get married, you need somewhere to live, and to get somewhere to live . . .

The dream dissolves, equation: fourteen-to-three-rooms, Pa's yelling, the brats, the image is suffocating.

Suddenly . . . No, it can't be him?

Hiding behind a lamppost, Moussa checks out a paunchy man of around fifty in his kamis and flip-flops, crossing the street. It is! It's Saïd, Z'hor's ex-husband, the bastard who kicked her out!

Moussa recalls his older sister's wedding, he really went to town. Money, music, the works. He loved Z'hor, everybody loved Z'hor. Djelloul had decorated the bridal car, a Mercedes he was repairing. He paid for the flowers. From his own pocket, he'd absolutely insisted. Good guy, Djelloul.

Then that bastard Saïd knocked her up, two kids one after the other, Maya and Fella. He made Z'hor wear the hijab, he beat her. She ran away at least a dozen times, until one day he threw her out, just like that. Justice of Islam. That's when Z'hor came back home with her two little girls. Saïd hasn't been seen since.

I'd like to smash his face in . . . Moussa watches him disappear around a corner.

A yellow and green Peugeot 204 pulls up. Taxi. Moussa suppresses his anger and leaps in.

Leather jacket, young, the driver pulls away and puts in a tape. Miracle: it's Stevie Wonder. Moussa thinks he's dreaming, settles back, and offers the guy a Marlboro. Do kids like this still exist in Algeria? Classy, sophisticated, modern—practically an Italian, for God's sake . . .

Driving up to the Hamma district, they talk, the cab driver's a singer, too:

"Yeah, we're getting a band together—jazz, blues, Western pop, for summer, get a contract, maybe gig on the coast, hotels . . ."

Moussa, rallying:

"I can help you, I know the manager of the Minzah Hotel, he's from my neighborhood."

The driver gives him his name and address. He's called Réda:

"That'd be great. But I wonder . . . what with the FIS and all that . . ."

Moussa flares up:

"What d'you mean, the FIS? They're just kicking up shit, that's all. They'll never get in. Run the country? They couldn't run a peanut stand, you've got to be kidding! And you think they're going to let them have their way? The Army, all that . . . No, it's all just bullshit."

Skeptical, Réda:

"Yeah, but they're armed, the attacks on the barracks

and the Blida court . . . and all the demos, there were at least a million of them last time . . ."

Moussa bursts out laughing:

"A million! Are you having me on? Why not a billion? Are you crazy? A hundred thousand, two hundred thousand, tops. Now the democrats' demo, yeah, I was there. There really were more than a million of us. Free Algeria, women, manager types, intellectuals, artists. Weren't you there?"

Réda changes up to fourth:

"Er, no . . ."

Moussa, warming up:

"You see? You've got to get out there. I tell you, we'll smash them. The FIS isn't the majority. What about the OK people, the managers, the workers, huh? They're the real Algerians, not that scum . . ."

Flipping over the cassette, Réda:

"Well, maybe you're right. What about you, what do you do?"

Moussa doesn't know quite how to describe himself:

"Um, I'm a singer, too . . . Kabyle. But not like the others, no. I don't do traditional, my style's more . . . Prince, Michael Jackson, you know?"

"Oh yeah, I'd love to hear you, and . . . have you already recorded stuff?"

"No, not yet. I'm biding my time. I don't want to do any old crap. I've had offers, but I'm waiting, I want to do it right."

Overtaking a truck, Réda:

"You're right."

Garbage bins, wasteland, Cité Mer et Soleil, the cab drops Moussa near a bunch of beards.

Holding the water pump, leaning against the tailfin, Moussa goes on chewing the fat awhile with Réda, then they part.

Does you good to meet people like that. Nice guy. You'd think there weren't any left in this fucking country.

Must get a set of strings for the mandola.

And . . . yeah, the meeting with the journalist, a nice little article's just what he needs.

Moussa skirts the puddle, clocks the group clustered near the garbage bins outside his building, and lowers his eyes as he walks in their direction.

Drawing level, he mutters a brief *Salam Alaikoum,* which they return with interest—the whole spiel about the prophet's memory: prayers and peace be upon him as well as upon his most august companions.

Moussa hurries toward the stairs, it must be one in the morning. A throaty voice calls him, it's Baiza, the former bus-stop mugger, the ripper.

Yeah, it's him all right. Baiza breaks away from the group and walks toward Moussa. Face furrowed by life's countless knocks, he was a brilliant soccer player once. Moussa remembers local matches: when Baiza had the ball, no way could you get it off him, a whiz, golden future in front of him.

But life . . .

Thrown out of school very early on, Baiza went off the rails. First, heavy drinking, then the lot: hash, amphetamines, fucked his head up. Arrested three times for stabbings, two six-month sentences.

A real viper, who's been using the mask of Islam as cover lately, Moussa knows. He hugs the water pump to his chest.

Baiza adopts the honeyed, caressing tones of Abassi Madani:

"Peace be upon you, brother. How are you? And your parents, and your poor brother Sahnoun, is he any better?"

Moussa tries to hit a *suitable* note:

"Yes, thank God. He eats, he sleeps, he's not aggressive, he's fine."

Stroking his hands, Baiza:

"Thank God, thank God. Your family's well respected, you always act in a godly way . . ."

Moussa, philosophically:

"We take things as they come, Baiza. 'We fall, we pick ourselves up again,' as the saying goes, that's life."

"Yes, 'Almighty God ties and unties knots,' it is His will. We are all in His hands. Tell me, I've been wanting to have a chat with you for a long time about . . . my concerns. Oh, only good things, all good things. Come, let's walk a little."

Puzzled, Moussa follows him. Baiza grabs his arm and steers him behind the garbage bins, out of the others' earshot:

"You know I've been worried about you for some time. I say to myself: Moussa's our brother, he has many qualities, he's loyal, sincere, generous, everyone agrees on that. What's more, he's educated, intelligent . . ."

"Thank the Lord . . ."

"Yes, thank the Lord. That's the truth that needs to be said. Only . . . you're missing just one thing . . ."

Moussa can see where this is going, knows these florid sermons by heart:

"What?"

"Oh, not much. You know, we really miss you at the mosque. We often talk about you, and, well, do you know what we said? We said that actually, if only you'd pray, you'd be perfect."

Moussa tries one tactic:

"But I pray in my heart, I keep Ramadan and I know 'that there is no God but Allah and Mohamed is his prophet'."

Baiza comes in for a tackle:

"'Blessings and peace be upon his soul.' That's good, no one doubts it, Moussa. Only . . . the way of the mosque will illuminate your life, God will protect you against Satan, and you'll see how the angels will speak to you . . ."

Weasel eyes creased, Moussa's convinced that he's off his head, typical look of someone stuffed with Valium and Mandrax.

"You're right, Baiza. But I don't feel it yet. I think about it, I'm sure it'll come. I'm still in the Shadows, I don't think I feel pure enough to . . ."

"Listen, that profession of yours . . . singer, it's not worthy of a true Muslim. Singing's for lost souls."

Looking at him squarely, Moussa:

"But a guy's got to make a living, Baiza, you know at home there are fourteen mouths to feed."

"It is God's will. I know all that, I know your family, we grew up together. But . . . how much do you make in your . . . career?"

How much does Moussa make?

"It depends, it's not regular."

Baiza, straight to the point:

"Listen, we made a decision at the mosque, we're going to find you a decent job so you can earn your living and keep your soul pure. On condition that you join us in our Jihad against the Shadows. What do you say?"

Moussa acts completely dumb:

"Oh, no problem! You know, unemployment, all that . . . can't say fairer than that. Beggars can't be choosers."

"We're going to find you a wholesome job—teaching, for example. We have lots of contacts, thank the Lord. Oh, and by the way, you'll have to have a word with your sisters. Thanks be to God, they're real women now. You must speak to them, gently, of course. Tell them to cover their nakedness. They must wear the hijab, and God will help them fight against Satan. Now, I'll let you get some sleep, I know we can count on you. See you soon, *In sh'Allah*."

"In sh'Allah."

They part, Moussa transfers the water pump to his right hand; the left's all clammy. Baiza goes back to the group by the garbage bins. Moussa heads for the staircase.

Can't escape from them. Ideally, it's best to come home around 5 or 6 a.m., then you can be sure there'll be no one around. One in the morning's still too early. I know how they all live, fifteen or twenty people in two rooms, sometimes just one. Spartacus's family of ten all live in one 200-square-foot room. Spartacus sleeps in the corridor, taking turns with his brothers. Has to, poor bastard.

Bristling with anger, Moussa climbs the stairs to the fifth floor, dodging a large rat on the way. He gently edges open the door, his forehead bathed in sweat, takes off his moccasins, and tiptoes to his room. Eurythmy of snores, fourteen souls in sleep's shadowy nets.

In the living room, Grandma, Saliha, Ouardia, Kahina, Z'hor, and little Fella sleep.

In the other room, Pa, Ma, and Nacéra.

An overwhelming urge to go up onto the roof terrace of the building and howl his weariness and bitterness to the stars. A brazier of tears fills his eyes.

He gets a grip.

Music, yeah, music's all there is.

Work, work, keep working. Become the best in Algeria, the best in the world, a diamond in the great firmament of the true, the greats. Moussa MASSY written in laser beams like at Prince concerts. Still with Fatiha, backstage.

The memory of Fatiha's eyes, green and tender, soothes his pain. Suddenly it's spring. Gleaming pearls of hope, like a saffron poem, streaming with perfect love down his skin, into his veins, rivers of gold. Fatiha, yeah, for her, it's all for her.

He navigates in the dark on tiptoe, don't wake anyone. In the corridor, three pairs of shoes. He puts his own with them and goes into the bedroom. They're all there, asleep, Sahnoun, Mohand, and Slimane. Each on his mattress on the floor, each pressed against his bit of wall, and little Maya who goes from one to the other, each night a different brother. Tonight she's sleeping with Mohand.

Moussa leaves the water pump in a corner, undresses, and slumps onto his mattress.

Sleep eludes him. Too much is too much. He lets his tears flow in the dark. His fists clenched, he weeps over his tattered life. Thirty-six years old and his life hasn't even really begun, not even married. Sleep gently starts to heal his pain, faces dance before his eyes, smiling, scented, Rachid, Farid, Sam, Réda, Fatiha. Just before he drops off, on the wall of his conscience he writes in big letters: stand up.

Three

Monday, 2 p.m., Ryadh El Feth, El Arika tea rooms in the Bois des Arcades, trendy haunt of the Algiers fast set. Perfect heat, royal sun, sky clear blue, the color of faded jeans.

Moussa's on the terrace. He's posing a bit while he waits for Fatiha. He likes posing in his Levi 501s, black Lacoste shirt, white sneakers, shades, and little silver chain bracelet, with his Dupont lighter and Marlboros lying on the table.

Butterflies dance around the honeysuckle bushes, the air shimmers, it's truly green, you can see a stretch of the bay from here.

A good day, in theory. A date with Fatiha, then meeting the journalist at 6 p.m. Could mean an article, you never know.

His gaze takes in the trees, the bay, Cape Matifou in the distance, La Pérouse. . . . Memories, military service.

The tables are all occupied, well-heeled youngsters, the scions of the Algerian bourgeoisie. They greet each other in French, rare these days in Algiers.

"Stop it, you're driving me nuts!"

"Hey, check out the chick in that car! Wow!"

The young jet set, the blithe insouciance of wealth, Mummy and Daddy take care of everything. The French lycée in Algiers, vacations in Lausanne, Los Angeles, Disneyland with Uncle Kader. Wolfing down enormous ice creams, whipped cream, raspberry, peach melba. Gorgeous girls, hair blowing loose, jeans and T-shirts direct from Europe, satin cheeks already tanned, chalet at the Club des Pins with Raouf and Aunt Nelly, going out for a drive in the Zodiac, eating grilled sardines bathed in the orange glow of sunset.

The car park's full—Mercedes, BMWs, convertible Golfs. Everyone knows everyone, an exclusive set, the offspring of ministers and generals—a powerful, gilded microcosm.

Trying to look cool, Moussa hides behind his shades and reads the newspaper, puffing on a cigarette.

He understands this world, no problem, but do they understand his? Rachid maybe, but even him. Rachid is different, it's true, he's lived a little.

He orders himself another coffee, the speakers blast out the instrumental version of "Your Song" by Elton John.

Moussa eyes the babes, inhales their perfumes, and loses himself in his newspaper again. Sports section: "Second round of the Algeria Cup, NAHD/CRB, the Algiers derby." Aye, aye, aye, it's all gonna kick off to-night, brother!

A silhouette appears on the terrace: long black hair, almond-shaped green eyes, polka-dot dress. It's Fatiha.

Moussa's heart sings, he waves, she comes over, kisses him chastely, and sits down.

Always the same feeling, those eyes shining, like the first time, candles of love, already five years ago . . .

Childhood friends from Cité Mer et Soleil. Fatiha when she was about thirteen, going down every morning with her brother Mustapha to buy the bread from Bouhar's. Two big loaves, five baguettes, and a large round *fougasse*, big yellow basket. Or with her short braids and red shorts, buying sardines from the itinerant fish seller every Thursday.

I watched her tranquilly, no idea at the time, little sister from the neighborhood, just a tender feeling. Actually, it was just after I came out of the Navy that it hit me, when I saw her after all those long months away. Purple spring. Around February or March, on a Monday afternoon. She was coming out of school with my sisters, I didn't recognize her, a real woman: pointed breasts, gleaming calves, crimson cheeks, yeah, that's when I looked at her properly. And me in parade uniform, the Navy, white short-sleeved shirt, midnight blue trousers, gleaming black shoes, peaked cap with braid and gilded stripes. Sergeant Boudjiri at your service, captain! She turned around and her laugh rippled out in the sunshine. She darted me a look with those green eyes that went straight to my heart. I was completely smitten, have been ever since. Fatiha.

The music switches to rai, the latest Cheb Hasni, "El Beida Mon Amour," flashy drum machines, good voice. Moussa:

"So, my love, did it all go OK?"

Blushing, Fatiha:

"Yes, the whole family was there. My uncle came over from France specially for the funeral."

From time to time she glances around, you never know, a brother, a cousin, a wagging tongue.

Calling the waiter over, Moussa:

"I remember your grandfather well, I had a long conversation with him once in Tizi Ouzou . . . He was very cultured, spoke perfect French. He recited Victor Hugo by heart. Yeah, the older generation . . ."

"He was one of the first Algerian primary school teachers, in 1920. That's quite something."

The waiter arrives. Arab vest and pants, old school. Curling his upper lip, he takes the order: pistachio ice cream for Moussa, strawberry for Fatiha.

Bermuda shorts, baggy striped sweaters, shades, a group of girls and guys are looking for a table.

◆

To think it's all thanks to Nacéra. She was the one who said to me one day: you know, I can see you two together. I was just thirty, the age when it's not so good to be on your own.

Thrown out of El Idrissi high school at fifteen, menial job at Telemly Post Office, a clerk. And then . . . no, there was no way I could carry on like that. I soon realized I'd had enough after six months, handed in my notice and all that shit. That's what Pa's never been able to forgive. After that, I said to myself, come on, keep cool, do your military service, get on with it. At least it's two years shut away from all the shit.

Fatiha came into my life right on time.

Actually, it was at Z'hor's wedding that it really hit me, which just shows that life, sometimes . . . you think that . . . and then bam, something happens. I sang all night, Fatiha was one of the guests. She came up to me at the end, in the garden, her eyes tattooed with love, the moon above us, gold on her hair, her face. That's when I said to myself: this is what I want, this is love.

A well-brought-up young lady, Fatiha stated her terms immediately: nothing before marriage. OK, that's only right, I agreed, anything for her, yeah, that's quite right, anything. Still, a bit of petting, checking out the goods, the rest's just craziness, fantasies.

But fantasies are good . . .

Getting laid's not a problem, there's always the girls of the night, skin on skin, in a stairwell, laundry room, cellar, on a rooftop, but it's not the same. No, no comparison. Fatiha is Fatiha, and that's all there is to it.

◆

A boy gives his girl a full-on French kiss. Shit, he's got a nerve! Moussa sees Fatiha's cheeks redden.

The waiter brings the ice cream, cool off. Moussa:

"Pistachio strawberry, that's green and red, the Algerian flag."

"But it's not really green, your pistachio, look . . ."

"True, it's almost blue, that makes it blue, white,

and red, France, Victor Hugo, de Gaulle. Why not? We Algerians are schizo."

"Mmm, it's delicious!"

Moussa gets straight to the point:

"I've missed you, you know, Fatiha. I haven't stopped thinking about you."

A respectable young woman, Fatiha takes refuge in her ice cream:

"Really?"

Moussa, changing tone:

"Yes, and you know, I've had enough, I want to marry you. I have to speak to your parents."

"But you don't have anywhere to live, Méziane . . ."

Only his family and Fatiha call him Méziane.

"All in good time, I'll be getting a place soon. Wait till I'm a little bit famous. Don't you believe in me?"

Fatiha smiles at him with her eyes:

"It's not that, Méziane. You know my parents, they're very strict on that. Whenever they talk to me about marriage, they always go on about having a steady job, an apartment, bank account, car . . ."

"So what? I'm no slacker! I make more than a banker or an engineer, and this is just the beginning . . . As a matter of fact, I'm meeting a journalist later on."

Alarmed, the beautiful Fahiha:

"But you're thirty-six years old, for goodness sake. And . . ."

"And what? So what if I'm thirty-six? Age has nothing . . . I'm going to talk to your parents, what do you say?"

Flustered with emotion:

"I . . . whatever you like, what do want me to say? You know best."

Two hours later, they leave the tea rooms and go for a walk in the Bois des Arcades, the only place where Algiers lovers have a little freedom. Illicit love.

Ryadh El Feth, a third-world answer to Paris's Forum des Halles. A massive, three-storey concrete mall, chic boutiques, movie theaters, art galleries, fancy restaurants, gyms, dance studios, the arts center, the Bois des Arcades. All built around the striking memorial to the dead: three giant intertwined leaves of concrete opening to the sky. The symbol of the three revolutions: industrial, agrarian, and cultural.

The esthetic of people's democracies, the same all over the world, fascism itself, caught between the *képi* and the turban.

Hand in hand, they walk down to the bus stop. Hand in hand's only possible in the Bois des Arcades, anywhere else it's forbidden, gossip, Islamists.

Moussa waits for the bus with her, watches her latch onto the crowd and vanish inside the bus, which pulls away immediately.

That's how it is, they see each other twice a week, nice. The rest of the time, it's hours spent on the phone, with secret codes. When she's with the family: it's going to be a fine day tomorrow means I love you. Their names change gender, too: Fatiha pretends to be talking to Habiba, a girlfriend. If he's talking to her, Fatiha becomes Habib, and that's how it's been for five years now.

Moussa doesn't dare hang around too long in Ryadh El Feth. Too much luxury, too grandiose for him, not his scene, no, not at all.

Now he has to go to Léveilley, meeting with the journalist at six o'clock. Yesss! Could mean . . .

✦

Taxi stand. Moussa only ever travels by cab, never the bus, too many people, his nerves, so he'd rather not. Mind you, he can afford it.

A tarpaulined Peugeot 404 honks at him. He turns around, it's Djelloul.

Moussa climbs in, Djelloul's just changed the carburetor, taking the car out for a test drive. Vulgar jokes, singing, thumping the door in time to the music as he drives. Djelloul drops Moussa in Léveilley, a nearby suburb sunk in poverty and Islam.

Moussa heads for the Dezdaza tavern, an improvised bar, no sign, no windows. Concrete and breeze block, a few tables, no chairs, you sit on beer crates. The place is teeming. Blinking, Moussa looks around for the journalist, everyone talking in loud voices, smoke, people pressed together like sardines. Eventually, Moussa spots him in a corner with two other guys.

Kamel Hamidi, cultural editor of *Algérie Actualité,* the weekly read by executives, the *Nouvel Observateur* of the Maghreb. Empty beer bottles all over the table.

Kamel waves to Moussa, introductions, Krimo, Fouad, colleagues from the *Nouvel Hebdo,* they all look plastered.

Moussa squeezes a buttock onto Kamel's crate. They

want to order him a drink, but the waiter's rushed off his feet, can't see a thing.

Dezdaza's the boss here. Mustache, built like a Turk, never misses a trick. Surrounded with customers, he sends the waiter over to their table. The waiter slams down a crate of beers in front of Moussa. There's only beer, and by the crate; they don't serve single bottles.

Each on his crate, the three journalists resume their conversation, the mysterious ways of politics, the FIS, the democrats, the Berberists.

Fouad, Trotsky glasses, thick mustache:

"The FIS comes out of the far right of the FLN. To piss off the left wing, the progressives."

Short, plump Kamel calms them down:

"Hold it, hold it, let me explain how it all works. It's the international reaction—the CIA, the IMF, and all that. Yeah, they're the ones that fomented the hotbeds of fundamentalism in the third world in the '70s. Why? Well, I'll tell you why: to fuck off Communism and the left, that's why. That's it. It's dialectic, they're behind the Saudis, why? Because it's all about profit! Oh yes, those Saudi bastards finance the fundamentalists through the CIA, and then there's oil . . . have you read that book by James Berg, *The Turban and the Well?*"

After four or five matches Krimo manages to light a Tarik:

"Yeah, but he's a Jew . . ."

Fouad breaks in, pushing his glasses up his nose:

"Come on, don't be stupid! Marx was a Jew, I'll have you know, and so were Einstein, Freud, and Newton.

The list is long. The guy's a Jew, so you switch off your brain? I reckon if the FIS wins the elections, the Army's bound to take power, don't you?"

Kamel retorts:

"Elementary, my dear Watson!"

Fouad, jamming his glasses on again:

"So, we have to choose between two evils: fundamentalist state and/or military state."

Moussa sips his beer, he's a bit out of his depth, but is fascinated by the discussion. Fouad buys some peanuts from a ragged kid:

Krimo tries to analyze the situation:

"But . . . the permanent emblems of nationhood—the flag, the national anthem, the Constitution . . . the Islamists don't give a shit about all that. They think they're ungodly. They've swept away the symbols of the Republic, desecrated the tombs of the martyrs of the Revolution . . ."

Fouad opens a beer wedged between his knees:

"That's their rallying cry. For them, there's no such thing as the notion of a republic, they've never demanded an Islamic *republic,* they talk about an Islamic state, which is different. For them, there is only the Umma, the Muslims' great motherland—in other words, a subjective given, based on faith. All the rest's unlawful. You should read El Mawdoudi."

Kamel, with a cynical look, smoothing his thick mustache:

"That moron? That's a load of crap! It doesn't stand up to analysis, it doesn't hold water for a second . . ."

Krimo, taking a swig of beer:

"Yes, but El Mawdoudi's their . . . bible right now. It's the whole basis of their ideology: Communism and capitalism have failed, so let's go for Islamism."

Kamel explodes:

"I don't like carrots, I don't like tennis, so I'll take the train. Where's the logic in that?"

Fouad, belching:

"Yeah, hence the systematic destruction of symbols, possessions, and materials that represent any form of power other than theocratic . . . Islamic, in this instance."

Kamel uncaps a bottle with his lighter:

"Back to carpets, oases, and camels, right?"

Fouad takes a slug of beer:

"Yeah, if you like. I know it sounds naïve, but it works, they're brainless. That's the real price we're paying. Thirty years of a fucked-up education system, it's a disaster. Algeria's one huge pile of rubbish sitting on top of a powder keg. That's the situation today."

Moussa's thrilled. He loves this kind of thing, listening to highly intelligent people analyzing the situation. He feels he's got something to bring to the party, too. He opens a bottle.

Two viewpoints emerge from the discussion. The first, expounded by Krimo, is that now that Chadli has legalized the FIS, it'll be Russian roulette. After the riots of '88 and the repression, ordinary people feel humiliated, so they're all going to vote for the FIS. You can't keep an Algerian down like that for long: rebellious and fierce, he'll bugger the ass out of your soul. *Képis* and beards will make strange bedfellows.

All this peppered with Marx, Che Guevara, Frantz Fanon, Gramsci, etc., of course.

Kamel and Fouad take a different view. They insist that in the FIS's own statutes, it's written in black and white that democracy's ungodly. Once the FIS is in power, it'll be the end of political parties, beer, and roses. They'll put all women under veils, it'll be total, ethical cleansing. There'll be no democracy. The fundamentalists will never get in!

The words sting Moussa's ears as he sits quietly in his corner, lapping up every word. He feels more sympathetic to the second point of view.

"Fundamentalism, are you serious?"

Krimo corrects him:

"Don't mix things up, I'm just trying to analyze, I'm not pro fundamentalism, dammit! But you've got to admit it's a major paradox . . . you legitimize the FIS, and then what? If they win the elections, what do you do with them? Abolish them? Play the game?"

Kamel, in very bad faith:

"There's no room for reason in this debate, that's where you're going wrong. Democracy itself's under threat, the country's going to hell, falling apart at the seams. There's no time to reason, we must act fast, crush them like bugs."

Moussa silently agrees, yeah, like bugs. He orders another crate.

Fuelled by the beer, the discussion grows heated, then veers into murky waters. I fucked the sub-editor in the john, the president of a women's association gave so-and-so a blow job in a car. Moussa's finding it hard to keep track, he can see they're each on their fifteenth or twentieth beer. He's thinking about his article, the interview, he's brought a beautiful photo of himself, shot and retouched by Rachid.

An article in *Algérie Actualité,* Algeria's biggest weekly, and you shoot to instant fame. To think there are so many morons who've wangled an interview, with pictures and everything.

Around 8 p.m., Fouad and Krimo stand up, got to go, shake paws, a real pleasure, see you soon, and Moussa finds himself alone with Kamel.

Totally blitzed, Kamel tries to pick up his packet of cigarettes, but drops it on the floor. Moussa retrieves it, no problem.

His speech slurred, Kamel:

"Thanks. Er . . . right, this interview . . . sorry . . . they're friends . . ."

"Oh, don't worry, I understand."

"OK, so you do modern Kabyle music? I really enjoyed your gig at the wedding the other day. Brilliant, what a vibe. A bit like Takfarinas."

Moussa hates being compared to Takfarinas. OK, he admits, he's one of the greats, OK, so he's a star, but he, Moussa, is different. He's doing something else, Prince, Michael Jackson. Try telling them that . . .

"Well, a bit."

Kamel's fumbling for his pen, Moussa offers him his. Kamel, smashed, drops it:

"Oh, sorry, I . . ."

Moussa picks it up and hands it to him. Laboriously,

Kamel looks for paper, pulls a dog-eared sheet folded in four from his billfold. An old summons from the city hall. The other side is blank, it'll do. He smoothes the sheet, his eyes streaming with alcohol:

"This'll be fine. It's all in my head, don't worry, I always work this way."

The interview somehow gets off the ground. Moussa describes his beginnings in '77, in the youth clubs, culturally under the thumb of the FLN, of course. The logo was two ears of corn, a tractor, a compass, and a bolt.

Then came the weddings and receptions. He talks about the early days and his influences—the great Akli Yahiaten, Idir, Enrico Macias, El Anka. He hears Rachid whispering exactly what he should say, image, style, promotion. He makes a point of slipping in Jimi Hendrix, the Beatles, explains his name a little, Moussa Massy, the whole concept.

Meanwhile, Kamel takes notes, crosses out, scribbles in the margin, it looks indecipherable, like a doctor's handwriting.

Moussa catches the waiter and orders another crate, might as well get this asshole really shit-faced. Moussa lays out all his cards, his ambitions, six or seven beers, feels good, the words trip off his tongue.

Everything comes up: nationalism, the recession, young people whose lives are fucked, Islamism, satellite dishes, everything Rachid's always telling him, got to invent a new music between Algeria and the whole planet, which will be One with Everything.

A magnificent phrase of Rachid's: "the universal is the local without walls"—Plato, I think.

Kamel's hand slips, spills his beer over the sheet of paper. Moussa grabs it and wipes it. The interview, for fuck's sake!

Kamel, the type to keep cool:

"It's OK, don't worry, I can still read it, go on, keep going."

The interview doesn't wind up until 11 p.m. Kamel folds the sheet of paper in four and slips it into his jeans pocket. He puts Moussa's pen in his shirt pocket, telling him it should appear at the end of the month, in two weeks' time.

As soon as he's alone, Moussa dances for joy in the street. An interview in *Algérie Actualité!*

Fuck it, this is fame! What's more, it'll coincide with the printing of Rachid's posters.

This is it, it's all happening.

I knew it from the start. In '77, just after the Navy, in the FLN youth club at the Parade Ground, there was that kid there, looked American, long hair, straight as silk, played guitar very well, sang the Beatles brilliantly, accompanied me singing El Hasnaoui's "Hula Hoop."

Well, what did that kid say to me? He said: "You, Moussa, you'll go far, you're a real star." I wonder what happened to him? Never saw him again, must have fucked off, more than ten years ago now. How time flies . . .

◆

The week the article's due to appear, Moussa's wild with excitement. He phones all his friends, his family.

Algérie Actualité comes out on a Thursday morning, for the weekend. Moussa spent the night before at Rachid's place, smoking, drinking, and fantasizing. Rachid told him he'd put together a press kit, two articles, that's good going, work on his look, presentation.

Then Moussa hung around outside, chain-smoking, reeling in the hours till daylight. At 6 a.m. the news kiosks open.

He pitches up at the kiosk outside his apartment building, his throat tight with suppressed pride. Shit, the whole building'll see my mug . . .

A newspaper goes far, circulation of more than a hundred thousand, it covers the whole country. Plus the embassies, the Algerian Consulates abroad . . . you're multiplied a hundred thousand times.

Old Salem's opened up his kiosk, black coffee, cigarette dangling from his lips, always dark tobacco without filters. Moussa composes his features into a neutral expression and walks up to the kiosk. Old Salem has his nose in a paper.

As soon as he spots Moussa, his face lights up:

"Hey, tell me, is that you in the paper, your photo and everything? Let me shake your hand, I'm proud of you, my boy. Moussa Massy, look, here it is . . ."

He shows him page 2 of *Algérie Actualité*. At once, Moussa sees the whole article, a good half page, with his photo top right:

"Oh, it's nothing, we do our best, Uncle Salem."

Old Salem, thrilled:

"Oh no, that's not nothing, your picture in the paper, just think! In the newspaper! You're a big shot, Moussa."

Pointing heavenward, Moussa:

"He's the big shot, Uncle Salem, the rest of us do our best. Here, give me ten copies, I need them, you know . . . contacts . . . work."

Clutching his ten copies, he races back home. Nearly 7 a.m., Pa, Ma, Grandma, Z'hor, Saliha, Mohand, Kahina, Ouardia, Nacéra, and the kids will be having their breakfast, the right moment.

He tears up the five flights of stairs and opens his front door. They're all in the sitting room, coffee and buttered slices of bread. Pa's silence reigns. Breathless, Moussa rushes in, everyone can see he's excited about something. Usually, he slinks straight to his room. Now he's standing right in front of them, all smiles. He says hello and throws the papers on the table, saying: page 2.

His sisters wriggle and grab the article, Grandma holds the newspaper upside down then turns it around for the photo. Utter amazement, exclamations, joy, Ma glows with pride, silently brushes away a tear. Only his pa says nothing. He examines the article, sniffing it all over, not quite believing it yet. He puts on his spectacles and looks from the photo to Moussa, comparing them and nodding, is doubly suspicious.

Moussa doesn't want to read it yet, no, he wants to be alone. He goes to his room. Sahnoun and Slimane are still asleep, there's a little light. Moussa's brought a cup of coffee with him, he props himself up against his wall, lights a Marlboro, and prepares to savor the interview.

He ignores the headlines: "Municipal elections on 12 June, FIS calls on voters to choose God." Moussa goes straight to his article, page 2, headlined: "Moussa Massy, the young hope of Kabyle music."

Photo's not bad, cropped a bit at the waist, but it's OK. Handsome, hair sleeked back, silk shirt, Berber vest.

Under the photo, a caption in bold: "In the footsteps of Takfarinas." Shit, Takfarinas again . . . that's all they can think of, dammit . . .

He skims the article, ". . . started out at the FLN youth club . . . sang the traditional songs of the Djurdjura . . ." but I never said that! ". . . celebrated the national culture as the vital, overarching binding force . . ." Don't understand a word, check with Rachid.

He reads the article four times in a row, holds onto the key words: "promising future" . . . "role model for young people" . . . "superb performer . . ."

A huge yawn, Moussa can't keep his eyes open, he puts the newspapers down on the shelf and crashes out.

◆

At 2 p.m., Fella comes to wake him, telephone, it's Rachid. He opens his eyes, still tired but blissed out. He feels like a different person, the article, everywhere, people will stare, but hey, that's fame.

Sahnoun and Slimane are deep in the article, each reading their own copy. Wordlessly, Sahnoun points to the piece, nodding, bursting with happiness. Slimane's more reserved, he keeps reading, stroking his goatee.

Moussa takes the call in the corridor, Rachid's bought

fifteen copies, too. He's over the moon, invites Moussa around to his place to talk promotion, career strategy, his image.

Moussa loves the buzz.

An hour later, he's at Rachid's. Heineken in one hand, joint in the other, Rachid doesn't hold back:

"Fuck it, finally they've taken notice. And about time!"

"Yeah, but did you see, they've got stuff wrong, and there are things I don't get."

Holding the newspaper, Rachid, cool:

"Don't worry, he's a wanker, that journalist, FLN type, I know his game. The main thing is the article, a hundred thousand copies, just think! A hundred thousand guys are going to look at your photo, it's like a concert in front of a hundred thousand people . . ."

"Yeah, you're right, it's . . ."

Rachid puts the newspaper down on the table:

"I'm going to cut it out and have it blown up. We should use a quote for the poster, just a phrase splashed across, it'll look good. Then we have to put it up everywhere, everywhere that matters, the Vincent bookstore, the arts center, in the colleges . . . Yes, this is going to work, I know it will."

Moussa listens, staring at his article upside down on the table. Rachid explains the obscure bits, the deeper meanings, the references, Moussa creases his eyes and nods, chain-smoking.

Four

A week later, 12 June, the municipal elections. The first free elections since Independence. Dozens of parties are contending, the walls of Algiers are dripping with posters. It's a bitter, anarchic struggle between all the parties except the FFS, which has called for a boycott.

Moussa, of course, didn't vote, convinced it would be rigged as always, 99.99 percent for the FLN, the famous "Continuity within Change."

At 8 p.m. the entire family gathers in front of the TV for the results of the polls. Visibly ill at ease, the female news anchor announces that the FIS has won a landslide victory taking three-quarters of Algeria's municipal councils. Even in the affluent districts, the well-heeled having spent the day at the beach.

Then a breakdown of the results by constituency. It's one long death knell, the FIS emerges triumphant almost everywhere, even in Kabylia.

The hydra's been legitimized.

At first Moussa laughs nervously, his knees tremble. No, it's not true . . . They're bound to say it's a joke.

Is this Iran?

Nacéra and Kahina start to cry, that's it, we're done for, they're going to force us to wear the hijab. Pa bawls at them to be quiet. Slimane's inwardly jubilant, Ma groans, her diabetes. Sahnoun's with the SAS.

Through the window, a mighty clamor echoes from every corner of the city. Moussa goes out onto the balcony and sees a dense moving throng, a vast black ocean. Hordes of bearded young men in kamis, thousands of them, in the grip of hysteria. Koran in hand, they chant verses and slogans: "Sharia now! There is no God but Allah."

Behind them, kids parading behind a barefoot, snottynosed self-appointed leader waving a makeshift flag, a torn plastic milk bag on the end of a long reed.

All around, cars honking, ululations, traffic jams. The FIS stewards zealously direct the cars. Moussa recognizes familiar faces: Spartacus, Baiza, Mustapha, Fatiha's brother. Look, even Slimane's down there, for God's sake. Going to have to sort him out, give him an earful, he deserves it.

Moussa doesn't want to see or hear any more. He goes back to his room to calm down and breaks out in a sweat. This isn't really happening?

What to do?

A chill runs down his spine. His mind's frozen, his limbs numb, his blood pressure plummets, he paces up and down. It can't be true? Better off sticking with the FLN in that case . . .

His mouth's dry, he goes to the kitchen and pours himself a glass of water. His grandma wearing a yellow and bright pink Kabyle dress asks him what's going on.

"This is it, the FIS has won, we're dead."

"Dead? The FIS, who's the FIS?"

Moussa goes back to his room and stares at the Michael Jackson poster and his own, side by side. Calm down, dammit. Yeah, the FIS'll be buggered. Carry on, work, work, work, hang in there. Music . . .

◆

The following Thursday, there's a wedding at Frais-Vallon. Late afternoon, usual briefing with the band. Sort out the set.

Djelloul's taking care of the transport. Pickup truck for the gear and the musicians.

Moussa rides in front, of course.

Djelloul's the band's official driver. He charges 100 dinars for each musician and has a good night out. Djelloul's never had a car of his own, he always drives the ones he's repairing.

Rachid should be coming. When Rachid comes, it's important, it's not the same.

Forgotten anything? No, set of strings for the mandola, found them at the last minute, black market. Stage outfit chosen with care, and the posters. Rachid's given him three, first proofs. He told him to put one on a display stand, clearly visible. Visibility is crucial.

Djelloul reverses into a parking space, puts on the hand brake, and turns off the engine. Everyone gets out, loads of people, cars parked haphazardly, kids. They're shown into a kind of dressing room—big cushions on the floor, smell of perfume, cakes.

On a side table is some Muslim whiskey—in a teapot, in other words. They roll joints, take slugs of whiskey, buff their shoes to a shine, tune their instruments.

Rachid chats to Moussa as he dresses in front of a huge mirror. He tells him about a video he saw on MTV and suggests ideas for Moussa's look. Moussa feels good when Rachid's there. Rachid knows his shit, fuck yeah, solid.

Dazzling in his green-spangled suit and leather tie, and fragrant with perfume, Moussa gives the band last-minute instructions, the sequence. Final adjustment to his bow tie, everyone looks immaculate.

Sound check, then launch into the first number. Vibe tense at first, audience on edge, the elections, shadow of the FIS?

Pouring all his rage into his mandola, Moussa goes straight for the gut, no messing around. Let's do it!

From the first song, the audience goes wild, men and women. They invade the dance floor. Moussa's on a high, he tries out different styles of song, different moves.

By the fourth number, he's Hendrix: he plays the mandola behind his head, on his knees, the crowd's in ecstasy.

Then it's the break, Moussa's in front of the mirror, checking his kohl, his teeth, his tie, his makeup. Everyone's congratulating him, that was amazing, thank you.

The bridegroom, wearing a tuxedo and white burnous, comes over in person to thank him. Moussa wishes him joy and lots of children.

In the mirror, Moussa looks himself in the eye. He

can see into the far distance, a faint green glimmer at the back of the cave. The smell of certain, early fame. Yesss, he's away.

Where's that joint got to, anyway? The bassist. Moussa:

"Hey, don't bogart that joint."

Bassist, doesn't quite catch what he says:

"Huh, what?"

Moussa, cool velvet:

"Bogart, Humphrey Bogart, you heard of him?"

Bassist, "Er . . ."

Moussa:

"You know, the '50s, Bogart, always had a cigarette in his mouth, he never passed the joint, get it? Don't bogart the joint."

Bassist, no reaction . . . Rachid chuckles quietly.

He got that one from Rachid, apparently it's an American thing, "don't bogart the joint," pass it on. Good old Rachid.

At last the bass player passes him the joint, Moussa takes two tokes, passes it to Rachid, and signals to the band. They're on again. Come on, boys!

He begins with a very gentle ballad, an old lullaby about mothers separated from their babies. Muted bass, light cymbals, bit of synth in the background, that's it. Moussa pitches his voice quite low, very ethereal, just on the verge of tears.

The emotion's overwhelming. All the mothers are dabbing at their eyes, wailing rises from the balconies. It gives Moussa goose bumps.

At the end, old women come on the stage to kiss him, to wish him long life, health, and happiness.

Now for the real deal . . . two, three, four, he gives the signal. "Ayadho," beautiful melody, lively, haunting chorus. It's going well, Moussa watches the bassist, the off-beat rhythm, gets the audience to clap their hands.

The second half's going better, the PA system's pretty much OK. Moussa has the audience eating out of his hand, is ruling the stage, he makes love to the mike, plays all his trump cards. The party goes on till the sun's already high, the first heat of the day. Moussa's tired but happy. He feels free, it does a guy good.

◆

Two weeks later, all the posters are printed, Rachid drove over to pick them up himself. Moussa on tenterhooks, meet up at Rachid's at 5 p.m. He's promised him some spliff to celebrate the event.

No problem, Moussa goes downstairs in his flip-flops and, from the entrance to his building, hails the first kid he sees, literally the first, and asks him to bring back 200 dinars' worth of gear.

Spartacus, leaning against the wall, beard and kamis, overhears. He walks up to Moussa:

"Brother, you looking for spliff? Listen, Dahmane got busted by the cops, but they didn't find the stuff, his wife had hidden it. Now she's selling it to pay for an attorney for him. If you want to do a good deed, in the name of God, she's got three kids, she's on her own . . ."

Feeling charitable, Moussa takes pity. OK then, he'll

take 400 dinars' worth. Braiding his goatee, Spartacus runs off to get him the gear.

On reaching Rachid's place, Moussa already feels plural: five hundred posters, just think!

Rachid's spread them all over the living room. MOUSSA MASSY, MOUSSA MASSY, MOUSSA MASSY everywhere.

"Take fifty or so for yourself, your friends, events, parties. We'll keep the rest for the day you release a cassette, and we'll add a sticker to promote it. By the way, have you thought about the title for the album?"

Moussa, excited:

"I thought of '*Zombretto*.' You know, the kids are all out of their skulls on *zombretto*. It's mother's milk to them. It's a title that reflects their world, their deprivation."

"Perfect, yeah, '*Zombretto*.' That's pretty cool. OK, let's go for it. '*Zombretto*, an album by Moussa Massy!' Yeah, and it sounds quite salsa, too. Cool!"

After two joints, a beer, they've got a plan of action. Rachid takes notes, turns on his computer, yeah, technology. Program, file, that's it, Moussa's knocked out by the computer, the mouse, it's a different planet. Rachid does projections, simulations, clicks on the mouse. Moussa watches his name come up on the screen, it's like NASA or something.

Shit, really got to make this work . . .

The plan's put together at last, Rachid's thought of everything, distribution, sniping . . .

◆

Moussa gave Spartacus three posters to put up around the neighborhood. At Bouhar the baker's, in front of the bus stop, on the wall of his apartment building.

Djelloul wanted one for his garage, Kahina for her supermarket, and Saliha, yeah, even Saliha, for her high school.

Moussa's put up four in his bedroom, plus another stuck on cardboard backing. Now he's a pro, he can start talking career a little, just a little.

And he'll have to up the rate for weddings.

At last, it's all beginning to come together. Little by little, not quite how he'd like it, but it's coming.

Moussa knows deep down he's not there yet, he's well aware it'll take more, a lot more. TV, mega concerts at La Coupole or Ryadh El Feth, on the esplanade, yeah, 50,000 people with at least a 60,000-watt PA. That means you've really taken off.

And then, the ultimate, of course: recording in a studio, releasing a cassette like everyone else. Don't settle for less, aim for the sky, beyond the horizon.

Part Two

◆

One

Le Tantonville café, near the old Algiers opera house. This is where singers and dancers hang out, showbiz types—nightclub, cabaret, and wedding musicians. This is where it all goes down. Moussa's becoming a familiar face. He comes here once a month, it's polite to put in an appearance, you never know.

Rachid's not too keen on Le Tantonville. They're a wild bunch, the Oriental music scene, deep-water sharks, nocturnal operators, whores, fights.

All kinds hang out on Le Tantonville's large terrace, spread out opposite Port-Saïd square: dealers, pimps, illegal taxis, pickpockets. Everything revolves around the music business. Look, even Bouras the conjuror is here with his tarty assistant Nadia, a bottle blonde who's been screwed by every clubber in town.

Moussa likes coming here—only from time to time, not too often, you've got to remain slightly aloof. Just to see the new faces, where things are at, who's playing with which band, equipment for sale, stay in the picture.

He sits down at a table of musicians including the old organist Mahmoud Aziz, highly respected pioneer of great Arab synth music. Moussa listens to him telling juicy anecdotes about the club scene.

At some point, a man comes over to Moussa and asks to speak to him in private. Intrigued, Moussa stands up, his antennae alert. No, don't know him.

He follows him inside and they sit at the bar. The guy turns out to be the brother of the boss of La Chésa, a club in Fort-de-l'Eau:

"I heard you singing at the wedding the other day. What a voice, my friend, what a voice! I talked to my brother about it, he agrees. We'd like to sign you up to sing at La Chésa every night."

Moussa's bowled over. A club? Professional?

His first ever contract. This is it, his career's taking off. Mustn't let his excitement show. Compose his face. Moussa:

"Well . . . I might be kind of available at the moment. Why not?"

They discuss the details. Start tomorrow if you like. Yeah, OK, how much? 200 dinars a night, plus tips, that'll make it 500. Then, if things work out, we'll see. OK, OK, start tomorrow, no problem.

The strange twists of fate . . .

Moussa leaps into action, rounds up the musicians, the equipment. He tells Rachid, who's thrilled. Posters, image, career . . . this is it, my old buddy, this time you're well and truly on your way.

◆

Twenty-four hours later, 8:30 p.m. Moussa's big night. The R5 Djelloul's halfway through repairing cruises into Fort-de-l'Eau, turns left slowly and parks outside the entrance to La Chésa. It's a beautiful night. The car doors open.

White linen suit, white tasseled moccasins, pink silk shirt, Moussa Massy steps out majestically, reeking of Fabergé. Overawed, the musicians follow and cluster around him.

Their first club gig.

A Camel between his teeth, Moussa arranges his fuchsia pocket handkerchief, adjusts his snakeskin tie, and flicks a speck of dust from his jacket collar. He smiles at them as he gazes at the rusty sign: "La Chésa," in pale neon letters with a leaping gazelle behind. The moon's blurred, and they can hear the pounding of the waves on the rocks.

ID check by the bouncer, Merzak, who shows them to the dressing room. The DJ comes to see them, explains the setup: mikes, interval, sets, dancers, the musical program. Moussa listens, trying to look blasé, seen it all before.

Don't show how excited you are, strictly forbidden.

Moussa reassures his musicians. Chill out. Let's go, Joe.

Music coming from the corridor, bossa novas, boleros. The Western musicians have started up. Not bad, must get to know them. Moussa and his band are on third, after the Oriental band.

Moussa comes out of the dressing room, glances around, poses. A few customers at the bar, smell of amber and detergent, the night's very young.

Moussa props himself up against the bar to be seen. He watches the band. Good musicians, especially the guitarist, quicksilver fingers, Rachid would like him, definitely. He'll be coming on Thursday with Lynd'.

The place gradually fills up, reserved tables with the compulsory bottle of Scotch, hostesses already in place. Jazzy signature tune, the band stops, time for the Oriental band.

Violins, derbouka, tambourine, organ, all full-on. The music's very loud and very shrill. Moussa can't take any more, he goes back to the dressing room. The boys are there, joking, smoking spliffs.

A heady whiff of perfume. A dancer comes into the dressing room, a creature of the night, ultra-short skirt, fishnet stockings, lips you want to nibble. She's beautiful, very young, tipsy, and already hard-boiled by the job. Hi, she's Warda, introductions, Moussa catches the look in her eye, seen it all before, don't even think about it.

Suddenly, she whips off her skirt, bustier, and panties, her voice husky with whiskey, tears, and cigarettes:

"You've all seen a naked woman before, haven't you? A woman's a beautiful thing, have a good look! I'll fuck you all with my big dick!"

She brandishes her arm like a phallus, wedging her elbow against her crotch. They all stare at her, dumbfounded, Moussa can't figure her out. Now Warda's completely naked, her breasts bouncing free. She strokes her belly, laughing. Then she pulls on her dance costume, beaded panties and bustier, transparent veil, tiara, copper castanets. Blowing a kiss from her fingertips, she vanishes.

Moussa takes it all in, etches it on his mind, the music scene . . . goes with the territory.

Half an hour later, the DJ walks over to them:

"OK, you're on."

Moussa checks his tie, one last glance in the mirror, gives the band a pep talk. Come on, boys, let's do it.

Harsh spotlights, the place is packed. Moussa adjusts the mike, they plug in their instruments. OK . . . three four, go!

At first, the sound's abysmal, no monitors, feedback, Moussa can't hear a thing. But despite that, people surge onto the dance floor.

Second song. Moussa gets pissed, tells the bassist to turn it up, the percussionist to play harder. Come on, guys!

Fourth song, the final thrust, Takfarinas's famous hit, "Way Thelha." Moussa loosens his tie. From the first notes, the audience recognizes it and erupts. Moussa goes down on his knees, that sends them wild, they're ecstatic. He almost sounds Hindu at times. He throws off his jacket, unbuttons his shirt, repeats the chorus again and again. Then he raises his arms for the finale, the killer. Roll of the snare drum, the percussionist's got it now, three, four, five cymbal clashes in sync with him, and Moussa leaps in the air, the final punch—and silence.

Standing ovation, very rare in a nightclub.

The DJ announces Cheb Krimo, the new young hope of rai music.

Exhausted, Moussa leaves the stage, staggered by the acclaim. A guy, forty-odd, wholesaler in plastic basins, invites him to his table. He's with two whores and another guy, customs officer. They congratulate Moussa, the whores giggle. They're on their second bottle of whiskey, 2,000 dinars a throw. After a few minutes, Moussa's bored with their slimy conversation—trafficking, money, guys on the make, boozehounds.

The rai singer's completely out of place, Moussa can sense it. One of the whores is openly making eyes at him, she's very young, not even twenty.

The joint's heaving now. The tables are crowded, pimps in turbans, jail fodder, Moussa looks on. Exhausted, he invents an excuse to retreat to the dressing room.

The DJ corners him and invites him into the booth, handing him a double whiskey. Moussa follows him in, checks out the equipment: mixing desk, red and green lights blinking. The DJ tells him about La Chésa in its heyday, the good old days of Salah Skikdi, and about the other clubs, La Houle, Le Santa Monica, Le Solitaire . . .

He tells him the hostesses' names, Samia Washbasin, Fatiha Gillette-blade, Nadia Belmondo. The drag queens, too, Rameses, Suzanne.

One of the hostesses comes into the booth, intoxicating perfume, heavy makeup, bottle blonde. She's brought the DJ a huge glass filled to the brim with whiskey. Paid by the bottle, they clobber the customer, pretend to drink, pour out large glassfuls, which they then pass discreetly to the guys. Ten percent per bottle, get them to drink and drink some more. It's a whole production line, come on, baby, I'm dying of thirst, buy a girl a drink.

The hostess straddles the DJ's knee. Moussa sees his chance and slips out.

On the stairs to the dressing room, Merzak, the bouncer, 265 pounds, pushes past him, throwing a customer out by the scruff of his neck. Merzak hurls him down the stairs, then beats him up, fists flying, occasionally pulling him up for a better swing. He finishes him off with a massive frontal head butt. Splat, the guy's out cold, badly cut above the eye, mouth full of blood.

Moussa's terrified, he's never seen that before. Merzak wipes the sleeve of his jacket and climbs back up the stairs. He slaps Moussa on the shoulder:

"Go on back to your dressing room. You didn't see anything, everything's cool . . ."

Wanting to puke, Moussa walks back into the crammed dressing room. The guys from the Western band are with his musicians rolling joints. Djelloul's keeping an eye on things. Moussa grabs a joint. Rabah, the quicksilver guitarist, makes a beeline for him:

"Hey, well done, your singing's fantastic. And it's nothing like Takfarinas!"

At last, someone who gets it. Moussa beams his most dazzling smile.

Around 5 a.m., everybody's out of it, the club closes.

The musicians move on to the Terminus. Coffee, sandwiches. Moussa likes Rabah, family man, great sense of humor, real Algiers kid, a regular guy.

◆

After that, it's routine, every night at La Chésa, except Saturday, day off.

It's well and truly summer, mid-July, blistering heat, the crickets' relentless rasping. One Saturday, Moussa decides to drive to the beach with Djelloul, in a pickup truck. Bahamas swimming trunks, Ambre Solaire, Madonna towel, shades, beach umbrella. Posing, yeah, even at the beach. Fatiha can't come to the beach, her parents and all that . . . pity.

On the freeway, a little cool air, doesn't do any harm. So hot! His shirt open, Moussa reads a page of the newspaper: "The FIS has banned the wearing of shorts in all areas." Are they mad? What're you supposed to do when it's more than 100 degrees in the shade? Wear anoraks?

Sickened, he throws the paper out the window and lights up a cigarette. When they reach the Club des Pins, Djelloul turns off to the right. Paying beach, classy, not too many jerks. The tang of the sea hits Moussa. The beach is really crowded, find a spot.

Djelloul spies a place near the water's edge, not far from the rocks. Perfect. The beach is a sea of colored sun umbrellas, a golden strip strewn with open flowers.

They plant the beach umbrella, spread out the towels, undress, and dive in, ooh, quite chilly at first. Moussa splashes about a bit, then strikes out toward the open sea, swimming breaststroke. Water's cleaner out there. What weather! Paradise.

He floats on his back. Complete and utter peace, the void. Children's cries in the distance.

Djelloul's lying on his towel, he dries himself reading an old copy of *Auto-Journal*. Fifteen minutes later, Moussa emerges dripping from the water, runs a hand through his hair, puts on his bracelet and gold chain. Are people staring at him? No, just a feeling.

The beach is full of bronzed girls, silky thighs, pert breasts. How old?

Moussa's utterly incapable of guessing the age of a girl in a swimsuit.

He joins Djelloul under the umbrella and pours himself a coffee. The radio, Spanish FM, the summer's hits, jingles. This is good. Yeah, this is the life. He looks at himself in his Elvis Presley pocket mirror, shakes the water from his hair, and combs it back. Mmm, the taste of salt on the tongue. He stretches out on his towel.

Beside him, a family's slicing a watermelon, kids play soccer, shit, the sand . . .

Lying on his stomach, Moussa feels the sun beating down. Ambre Solaire, smells good, smells of money. Djelloul rubs some more into his shoulders.

Dirty ragged country kids are selling dubious-looking doughnuts. Why do they have to come to this particular spot? They're spoiling the view.

Djelloul's secretly in love with Nacéra, Moussa's sister. Has been for years. Moussa soon noticed his keen interest in the family. First of all swapping thrillers with

Sahnoun, then repairing Saliha's car. After that, turning up for all the major events in the family's life—funerals, weddings, births, Djelloul's always been there.

When did I guess?

I think it was one day when we'd driven Nacéra to college. Djelloul was red as a beetroot, didn't say a word the whole journey. Sure, my little sister's cute, with her chubby cheeks and you-want-it-you-got-it smiles. Twigged immediately, no need to spell it out, but I never got involved. Oh no no no, no way, too delicate, these things, it's up to them. I don't think Nacéra realizes, unless she's playing hard to get. It's deep and . . . all that stuff . . . women, you never know whether they really mean what they say. Wonder if they'll get it together. They're not in the same league, I mean . . . Nacéra's at college, whereas Djelloul . . . yeah, well, that's life . . . Tomorrow it's back to the old routine, La Chésa, the girls, the fights, not exactly what I thought. Rachid came on Thursday, dropped in with Lynd', God, she's gorgeous, Lynd', looks like the girls in *Dallas*. I bought them a bottle of Scotch, 2,000 dinars. No, no, whatever it takes, have to, never stint when it comes to Rachid. It's the first time Rachid's set foot in a cabaret club. He was pissing himself laughing, it reminded him of the old American movies, '30s dives, the pimps, the whores, the suckers. He really liked the Western band, especially Rabah the guitarist.

At La Chésa, there's a tiny staff kitchen behind the bar—sandwiches, fried eggs, and so on. In the interval,

I took Rachid in there, and we bumped into two dancers and Tikechbila, the Moroccan singer. He was drunk and stoned out of his mind, trying to fry himself an egg. When he put the pan on the gas, he dropped the egg on the floor, all black with grime, puddles, cockroaches. The egg broke. Rachid and I sat and ate our sandwiches, ground beef with onions. Tikechbila didn't say a word, but got down on all fours and sucked the raw egg from the floor, slurp, just like that. Then he stood up and thumped his chest, yelling like a gorilla.

I put down my sandwich, thought I was going to puke. Rachid was doubled up with laughter, it didn't bother him. Slice of life, as he says. Good old Rachid.

Moussa buys a dodgy doughnut from a dodgy kid. Oh look, Djelloul's coming back, he's been an age, went off to buy ice cream. A cone in each hand, he's stomping through the sand.

Moussa takes a lick. Not bad this ice cream, vaguely strawberry. Oh, this is the life!

If everyone stopped pissing around with the FIS, politics, the black market, all that shit, we'd be a normal country, like any other. Good morning, sir, thank you very much, after you, have a nice day. Instead of . . .

It was Ibn Khaldoun, or I don't know who, who said: the Arabs agreed never to agree. Well, he wasn't wrong, old Khaldoun . . .

Five o'clock, time to get going. Pickup truck, pack up the gear, the umbrella, the towels. Before getting into the truck, they brush the sand from their shoes and clothes, get dressed, and check their tans. Not bad, caught some sun, though Djelloul's naturally dark already.

Back to the fold. Driving through the coastal villages, Moussa stares at the people, kamis, beards, FIS banners, verses from the Koran. Don't even know how to enjoy the sea, should live in the desert, oases and all that, yeah, like the Bedouins. That's it, they can have the desert, perfect for them and their fucking Islamic state, then they can leave the rest of us in peace.

Still very hot. Moussa's stripped to the waist, fanning himself with the towel. At the exit to Staouéli, police roadblock, the cops signal to them to pull over to the right. Odd.

A young cop, face contorted, beads of sweat on his brow:

"Tell me, why do you think I stopped you?"

Moussa has no idea, everything's in order, lights, papers . . .

"I don't know."

The cop, poking his head through the window:

"Offense against public decency. Is that any way to dress? Do you often walk around naked in front of your sisters, your mother?"

Moussa, calm:

"No, it's the heat, I'm not naked, I . . . it's only my shirt, I was just about to . . . Excuse me, I . . ."

"Get out of the car and follow me."

Keep cool, don't annoy him. Moussa buttons his shirt up to the collar and follows Djelloul and the cop to the station. Shabby duty office, flies, smell of mold, fat,

grimy log book on a table, butts spilling from the ash-
tray, dusty portrait of Chadli on the wall.

Djelloul and Moussa stand there, the cop walks
around them, his hands behind his back:

"What's your job?"

"Er, singer. Weddings, parties . . ."

His nostrils quivering, the cop comes up to him, staring at him closely:

"Singer? Tell me, is that kohl around your eyes? You
wear makeup as well? Are you a faggot by any chance?
Filthy degenerates . . . so, you're a singer?"

Djelloul and Moussa stand to attention. Cold sweat,
keep a low profile. He's armed, you never know. Silence.

A resounding punch floors Moussa. The gendarme:

"Answer my questions, you little faggot!"

His lip bleeding, Moussa:

"I . . . got to earn a living, there are fourteen of us in
three rooms, and . . ."

The cop kicks him on the shoulder and draws his gun.
Moussa turns ashen. He's suddenly freezing cold.

"Shut the fuck up, you queer! If I had my way, I'd
wipe out the lot of you, you little pile of shit. Suck the
barrel, go on suck it, you like sucking, don't you?"

He puts the barrel to Moussa's lips. Moussa, wounded,
sucks the cold barrel, weeping. The cop yanks him up
and stares closely at him, taking in the bracelet, the gold
chain. Moussa can feel his fetid breath on his cheeks:

"You must be a faggot, or if not, you run after honest
citizens' wives. I know your kind, filthy little shit."

At this point, a second cop comes in, a superior:

"What's going on?"

The cop:

"They failed to show me respect, lieutenant: insulting behavior."

The superior questions Moussa, who doesn't dare deny it. He ties himself in knots apologizing.

The superior's had enough, late in the day, heat wave:

"Right, fuck off out of here quick. Next time you insult an officer of the Law . . ."

Djelloul and Moussa nod. Sniggering, the cop shows them out. On the way he surreptitiously sticks the barrel of his pistol up Moussa's ass.

Once outside, they clamber into the pickup truck and drive off. Moussa begins to sob, banging the glove compartment in rage. Djelloul consoles him, they're assholes, motherfucking power freaks.

The randomness of it. It's not the first time. That's why I got involved in the mother of all riots in '88, with the kids, mindlessly smashing everything, I clearly saw the Army fire into the crowd, at boys. Before my eyes, that boy barely fourteen years old standing on a car hood. I saw a soldier take aim and shoot him with a machine gun, a 12.7, that hurts. A long burst, that can do some damage. Yeah, saw the kid sliced clean down the middle, a gazelle in full flight.

On reaching the project, they part company. Moussa climbs the five floors picking his way through the brats.

In the bathroom, there's no water. Jerrican, basins. He washes, rinse off the salt, clean up the blood, his lip's badly cut. Fucking country, the injustice, all he wants to do is get blasted. Rachid's not around, pity, he's in Barcelona visiting his aunt.

◆

The next day, Moussa goes back to work, but his heart's not in it. La Chésa, it's a cutthroat scene, nothing like what I was expecting. This isn't the road I want to go down, this is shit. But, as Rachid says, got to learn the ropes, hang in there, take the long view.

Forget the cop. Moussa starts drinking early, around 6 p.m. He goes onstage completely off his head. Can't see straight, perfect that way.

That evening, he sings like a god, weeping real tears. Rabah applauds and whistles, everyone's on their feet, people jostle, slip notes inside his shirt collar. When his set's over, Moussa goes straight to his dressing room, roll a joint quick, get stoned, blot it out.

Warda the dancer's openly infatuated with him. Be careful with these women, bunch of vipers, jealousy, hassle.

Moussa remains impervious to her advances.

One night at closing time, on leaving the club, one of the Oriental musicians approaches him. Taking him by the arm, he says he wants to talk to him. Moussa follows him outside the club, where the illegal taxis are filling up with club staff, dancers, musicians.

It's already dawn, blue sky, sea just to their right, the shimmering golden sands. The musician suddenly pulls an axe out of his shopping bag and lunges at Moussa:

"You bastard, I'll hack you to pieces, you dare try to fuck my wife in front of my eyes?"

He's Warda's guy.

Panic-stricken, Moussa runs and hides behind the cars. Everyone's staring, but no one gets involved. Woman trouble, best keep out of it.

Moussa stumbles and falls, the other guy brandishes the axe over his face. Suddenly, Djelloul comes racing over clutching a mike stand. With a howl, he stuns the musician with three violent blows. Then he holds him down and beats him around the face:

"You fucking leave him alone, right? Or I'll fuck your face up so bad your own mother won't recognize you!"

The musician, swollen-faced:

"I'll kill him . . . wherever he goes, I'll kill him . . ."

On this magnificent June morning, Moussa watches the musician's blood seep into the warm sand, red on gold, seagulls cutting through the clean air.

◆

A few days later, Moussa buys himself a flick-knife. If anyone comes near me, I'll use it. Simple.

La Chésa, routine. One evening, someone comes into the dressing room and asks for him. Respectable-looking, a cut above the usual customers:

"Bravo, that was great. Listen, I work at Le Triangle in Ryadh El Feth. I'm here with the artistic director. We'd like to talk to you."

Le Triangle? That's the biggest club in Algeria, a mecca for the in crowd, the chic set. Everyone in Algiers talks about it. Moussa's never set foot inside, not his scene.

Rachid, yeah, he's a regular, often mentioned it.

Moussa follows the guy to a table where two others are waiting. Introductions, a foreigner, sound engineer apparently, and the artistic director.

Just from his appearance, Moussa can tell that this is whole different ball game. Bill, the artistic director: attractive, long hair, white pants, green Lacoste shirt. He offers Moussa a drink, immediately puts him at ease.

Moussa warms to Bill at once. Calm, self-possessed, laid-back, definitely a Westerner. But what the hell are they doing in this crappy joint?

Gradually, they get to the point. Bill:

"Yeah, your repertoire's good, it's new, nothing like Takfarinas . . ."

Really? That's the second time. So there is a God after all . . .

"Thank you, it's kind of you to say so. I do what I can."

"Yes, very original, your look, your act. And also . . . good idea, your poster outside, very professional. I like people with ambition. It's good, given your repertoire, yeah, the '50s, El Hasnaoui, all that. You don't hear that stuff very often."

Introduce him to Rachid, be perfect together, the cream of the fine Algerian race.

As normally everyone should be, shouldn't they! Moussa feels himself coming alive again, so much consideration, genuine attention:

"People have forgotten El Hasnaoui. I think he was ahead of his time singing "L'Aéroport" or calypsos like "Hula Hoop" in the '50s. That took guts . . ."

"I absolutely agree. Listen, we're looking for fresh talent for the lineup at Le Triangle. I want something creative, new. I've had enough of those exec types, they're all sharks. If you're interested, we could work something out. Here's my card, give me a call. You can start when you like."

It's just when you think there's no hope that life can give you a happy slap, bang in the middle of your face. Wham, just like that.

Le Triangle: didn't even figure in Moussa's dreams, it's so . . . and now? Bill who . . . wants to sign him up, on the spot . . . Moussa takes the elegant business card, gilt lettering on a black background:

"Er, I had no idea . . . it's . . . I wasn't expecting . . . I'll have a think. I'll call you very soon."

Bill gives him the lowdown on Le Triangle, a different class of audience, the favored stomping ground of the elite. He mentions in passing that the contract's only for Moussa, and not for his band. Le Triangle's own musicians are excellent, they accompany all the stars. Bill drops a few names: Abdallah, Hamid, Mahmoud Aziz, Algiers's finest, the leading lights of modern Oriental music.

Ouch, problem: the musicians, his buddies, how's he going to tell them? That's a tricky one. See Rachid, must be back from Barcelona, discuss it with Djelloul, in confidence.

Moussa buys them a round back and goes off to play the second set, half floating on a cloud of gilded joy.

On the way home with Djelloul, Moussa tells him everything, asks what he thinks.

Djelloul's beside himself:

"Le Triangle? Shit man, that's it! You've done it! Yeah! Fuck it, you've made it!"

Moussa tells him about the slight hitch: without the band, his loyal friends, his brothers in times of hardship.

Djelloul, philosophical:

"Right, yeah, problem. But . . . that's life, Moussa, every man for himself, each to his destiny. You're not going to carry them for the rest of their lives, what would they do in your shoes?"

That's true: what would they do in my shoes?

The next day, the phone rings, it's Rachid, back from Barcelona. Moussa tells him the whole story.

Rachid whoops: "Waheyyy!!! I knew you'd make it. But so fast . . . don't even think twice, Moussa, not for a second, it's a once-in-a-lifetime chance. Besides, I know Bill, he's brilliant, a real artist, a jazz musician too. Go for it, explain to the guys, they'll have to understand."

Heartened, but at a loss, Moussa wonders how to break it to them. It's a nightmare, how will he tell them?

Rendezvous in a café, Moussa tells his musicians the news. They sit there speechless. After a brief silence, the reaction's divided.

The organist and the bass player understand, wish him good luck, yeah, that's life, we'll play together again some day, who knows?

But the percussionist and the violinist take it badly: what's going to happen to us, and the repertoire we've worked so hard on, you can't just ditch us, you selfish bastard . . .

Moussa takes it, understands, what can he say? It's a wrench for him, too, leaving them. So many memories, the hard slog, the parties, their shared musical dreams . . .

They part, their hearts constricted. It's the end of something, the beginning of something new, things are moving forward, that's the main thing.

Moussa calls Fatiha, too, to tell her the news. At first, she's excited: Le Triangle, who in Algiers hasn't heard of it?

But immediately she changes her tune. Jealousy, beautiful women, you're going to forget me, they'll turn your head.

Moussa reassures her, she's the only one he cares about. He reminds her of his oaths of love under the moon. It's been five years, their love affair, this is it now, the light at the end of the tunnel. Le Triangle, fame, it's all within reach. Money, fame, a place to live, marriage . . .

◆

The following month, he gives a week's notice at La Chésa and calls Bill to tell him he's ready.

Moussa plows all his earnings into clothes, everyone knows that. But this is something else: Le Triangle isn't La Chésa, you've got to look really professional. A new wardrobe, check out Lâkiba, the luxury black market.

It's expensive, but essential, you've got to nurture your image.

Once a month, Moussa mooches around Lâkiba, rummages through clothes, knickknacks from *over there.*

Torment of Tantalus, most people don't buy, just come to drool, can't afford it. Western goods spread out on the ground—perfume, soap, religious baubles, batteries, porn videos, gadgets, vendors vying with each other in their banter.

The prices hurt, but Moussa doesn't care. He tries on a black silk shirt, caresses the fabric, beautiful material, puffed sleeves with two false pockets. Fantastic.

Ferreting some more, he spies a pair of Hindu-style canvas moccasins, embroidered with colored beads. OK, he bargains, how much for both? Fifteen hundred it is. Moussa takes the shirt and the shoes wrapped in newspaper. Excellent for his debut at Le Triangle, goes with the image of the place. Later, we'll see. It all depends. Yeah, it'll be OK.

In passing, he buys a stick deodorant, 150 dinars, probably 5 francs at Tati, but who cares: smelling good's important.

Two

Beginning of August, suffocating heat. Meeting with Bill at Le Triangle at 3 p.m. to finalize details, rehearse.

Djelloul drops Moussa in front of the arts center. Shades, Batman T-shirt, gripping his mandola, gets his bearings.

Ah, not so hot here. Air-conditioning, cool concrete, everything's clean, wonderful smelling. Just like *over there* . . .

Going down to the bottom level, Moussa notices the luxury stores, the beautiful, perfectly groomed women. This could be Geneva. People sitting at tables on the café terraces, girls and boys. The sweet air of wealth, normal life, I guess.

He clocks the security guards: discreet, walkie-talkies, uniformed, clean. They're right, all this needs protecting from the scum.

Moussa can hardly walk, it's all so pristine. Cleaning service, cute little garbage bins everywhere, designer public ashtrays. Goddammit, it ought to be like this everywhere.

On every level, TV monitors broadcast endless videos, foreign channels. Moussa can't get over them. He stops for a second or two. The picture, sound, colors, they're all perfect. It's funk, with chicks in sexy shorts singing the chorus. He watches the ads, too. Life is sweet.

Pa's against satellite TV, he thinks it's too . . . which means no, he won't have it, and that's that.

Moussa finds Le Triangle on the ground floor. The place looks closed. But Bill said 3 p.m., didn't he? Moussa peers through the window. Someone comes over, jeans and flip-flops, yawning. It's a bartender, migrant worker. Moussa asks for Bill and the guy lets him in.

Le Triangle's a massive great bunker. Cleaning women in the huge lobby, vacuum cleaner, floorcloths, it's nice to see. The bartender directs Moussa to the left. He can hear music.

Bill's supervising a rehearsal. He motions Moussa to come over. Onstage are Abdallah the bass player, Hamid the percussionist, and Mahmoud Aziz, the organist. They're all yawning, hungover from the night before.

Bill introduces Moussa. They all know each other by sight. The musicians are rehearsing a new song with a female singer from Constantine. Notepad in hand, Bill's scribbling her songs, the changes. He asks Moussa to wait.

Moussa sits down in a corner and watches. They're real pros, perfect-sounding PA system. Bill mixes the sound himself. Ammar the DJ's cool. He shows Moussa around the place while he's waiting for Bill to finish with the others.

Le Triangle has three spaces, the disco, the Oriental club, and the jazz club.

First, the disco. Moussa's never seen so much equipment in his life: lighting booth, mixing table, video equipment, CD players. The room's massive. Ammar shows him a giant speaker, it's taller than Moussa.

Bet that sounds awesome, fuck!

Then the jazz club. Very intimate, twenty or so tables, American bar, small stage, drum kit, electric piano, amps. Moussa notices the spotlights. There's a fantastic glass roof, a/c, sound booth, state-of-the-art equipment, mixing table, sound system, tape decks.

Lastly, the Oriental club: as big as the disco, "exotic" décor, big stage, well-lit dance floor, lighting system.

Bill's just finished with the female singer, now it's Moussa's turn. He takes out his repertoire, the musicians try out the songs. They get the chords straight away. They're good, that's for sure. In two hours, the whole thing's done and dusted. Work the rest out as we go, get a good flow, all that.

Bill buys Moussa a drink and tells him the hours, the dress code, the importance of professionalism. Le Triangle's a showcase for the authorities, a playground for their children, have to tread carefully.

Le Triangle opens at midnight, formal dress, unaccompanied persons not admitted. Moussa's slot is at a quarter to one in the morning. It's nearly 6 p.m., time for a nice long siesta, recharge.

His head filled with dreams, Moussa goes home, slips into bed, and tries desperately to sleep—got to, until 9 p.m. at least.

Sahnoun's deep in a detective novel.

But no way can Moussa sleep with doors banging, the old man yelling, the TV bawling. At this hour everyone's coming home from work, from college or the streets.

Irritated, Moussa gets up and goes into the bathroom. He improvises earplugs from cotton wool—it's better than nothing. He manages to drift off.

Nine o'clock. Get up, eat well. He saunters into the kitchen and Z'hor serves him a hefty portion of chicken couscous. Mohand comes back from the living room chomping on a slice of watermelon:

"Hey, don't see much of you these days, night owl. What are you up to?"

Moussa tells his big brother about Le Triangle, his career. Mohand listens, nodding, still attacking his slice of watermelon:

"That's good, you're on the way up, you'll make a lot of contacts there."

"Yes, and for your wedding next year, I'll get you the biggest stars in Algiers, they're all at Le Triangle. By the way, any news on . . . an apartment?"

Mohand stops chewing and spits out a seed:

"My file's still on someone's desk at the Ministry of Trade, social affairs subdivision."

"Don't you know anyone there?"

"Yeah, I know the deputy director's neighbor. He promised me he'd put in a word. I even offered him money."

Moussa, feeling sorry for him:

"I can help you out cash-wise, but that's all I can do."

"Thanks. I've got to get married next summer what-

ever happens, Moussa. Her parents won't wait any longer. We've been putting it off for three years now, it's not
right. They've had enough, and I can see their point."

Polishing off his chicken leg, Moussa ventures:

"And . . . how? Are you going to . . . live here if they
don't give you an apartment by then?"

Mohand puts down the rind of his watermelon slice
picked clean:

"What can I do? We'll have to manage somehow.
Look, I'm forty-five. Am I ever going to marry?"

He walks out of the kitchen. Moussa finds it hard
to swallow the rest of his couscous at the thought of
Mohand marrying and bringing his wife back here. How
on earth will they fit her in? Fourteen, no, that'll make
fifteen people, and they'll be married, so they'll need
their own room, won't they?

But how, there are only three bedrooms . . . for
fifteen.

Unless Maya or Fella . . . or Grandma?

Fucking shithole. It does his head in thinking about
the various permutations. He leaves the kitchen, wants to
get back in his bubble, where he can breathe.

In the bedroom, he notices an FIS sticker on the wall.
He rips it off in a fury. It has to be Slimane—got to have
some serious words with that asshole. The FIS in the
house, that's going too far.

No, no, no.

Slimane comes into the room, kamis, goatee, flip-
flops. Moussa looks him up and down and points to the
sticker:

"Did you stick that shit on the wall?"

Turning red, Slimane stares at the floor. Moussa raises his voice:

"Answer me when I speak to you!"

Sahnoun looks up briefly from his novel, then goes back to it, unperturbed.

Slimane tries to explain:

"I . . . it was Baiza who gave it to me, he said . . ."

Moussa begins to yell:

"Look, I've been meaning to talk to you about all this, those guys you hang out with, the fundamentalists. So Baiza's an authority now, is he?"

At the sound of Moussa shouting, everyone comes running, Z'hor followed by Nacéra, Ouardia, the kids. Mohand doesn't want to get involved. Grandma comes to Slimane's defense:

"Leave the boy alone, he hasn't done anything wrong."

Moussa, beside himself:

"What?! The FIS in our house? Is this Iran? Are you all mad? And in my bedroom! I forbid him to hang around with them. If he wants to pray, he can pray at home. He won't learn anything about religion from that scum!"

Slimane's red with shame. No, he's not really a true Islamist, just a vulnerable social reject, a fallen blossom, easy, impressionable prey.

Moussa won't stop shouting. Everyone leaves the room. Sahnoun appears not to have seen or heard a thing, still absorbed in his book.

Moussa wants to throw the sticker over the balcony,

but changes his mind. Suppose he bumps into the Islamists that hang around outside the apartment building?

He doesn't know what to do with it, so he stuffs it in the pocket of his torn-at-the-knees jeans. Throw it away outside later, dump it discreetly in a garbage bin.

Get a grip, it's nearly 10 p.m. Djelloul's coming at 11:30, first night, mustn't be late. Moussa insisted on having Djelloul as his driver, that way he gets in for free. Bill said no problem.

Right, got to get ready. The big communal closet. Moussa can't make up his mind what to wear. Got to get it right, this is Le Triangle, not La Chésa.

He chooses the black silk shirt, a white vest with embroidered false buttonholes, baggy white serge pants, and the shoes.

Problem, the shoes: he can't decide between the black braided moccasins or the ones with the gold ring on the side. Come on, make up your mind, heads or tails. Right, it's the moccasins, no argument.

He locks himself in the bathroom for a proper session. Moussa fills the huge basin with water from the jerrican and washes, using a bronze bowl to pour the water over his body. He washes his hair with what's left of the Dop shampoo, 120 dinars on the black market.

Rinse thoroughly, comb back, and wind tightly in a towel. Leave for ten minutes. The '50s look. He smiles at himself. Moussa the Pharaoh.

Then, a close shave and vigorous rub with William's aftershave, black market, 160 dinars.

Moussa MASSY the star. His face an inch from the

mirror with the Z-shaped crack, he preens himself: plucks nostril hairs, squeezes blackheads, white smile, says "cheeese" several times. Rachid taught him that: repeat several times for smiles to camera.

Let the aftershave do its work, slip on the shirt, cool silk soft on his skin. Then the white pants, the little vest, shoes later on.

Now for the hair, the crucial last stage. Carefully remove the towel, a blob of gel and brush vigorously. Allow the gel to penetrate every hair. Then, take the wide-toothed comb, and gently sculpt the locks, the curls. It's all glossy, beautiful, shimmering fantasy.

Moussa loves the moment when he gazes into the mirror and inspects his work. Romantic curls on the nape of the neck, hair plastered down smoothly at the back with just two tiny side waves and a little kiss curl on the forehead.

A hint of kohl around the eyes. He stares at his three-quarter profile, bursts out laughing, poses. Who's the star of Algiers? It's good. Perfect.

Honking outside. Moussa strains to see over the balcony. It's Djelloul, must be 11 p.m. Better get a move on.

A generous spritz of Azzaro under the arms, cigarettes, ID, cash, keys, sorted. Moussa goes out, down the stairs, hitching up his pants. Avoid the piss puddles.

Bunch of beards in the lobby. Shit . . .

They all stare at him, he reeks like a whore. I know what they must be thinking . . . Walk past, curt *Salam Alaikoum,* the beards reply just as curtly. Change tactics, better not attract attention in this getup, you never know.

Djelloul's wearing a suit and tie, the big night. He stinks of aftershave, too. He has a BMW today. As Moussa gets in, he says he hopes Djelloul will have his own BMW one day.

Ryadh El Feth, restaurants, movie theaters, cafés, bright lights, luxury cars, women just like in the movies. Parking lot, Djelloul finds a space and they get out.

There's a crush outside Le Triangle, ruthless door policy. Members with cards first, then regular customers and reservations. You can't just walk in off the street.

The chicks are dazzling—tanned to perfection, all aglitter. Moussa spots Bill next to Lounès, the bouncer. Bill introduces them, new artists, Lounès memorizes their faces, OK.

Loud music from the disco, it's already bursting at the seams. Moussa feels lost in the lobby, Djelloul's behind. A chick comes out of the disco, Moussa stands there slack-jawed. She looks like Kim Basinger, never seen a woman like that in his life. He sees another, Afro supermodel type, and another, '30s look, holding a long drink, and another, and another . . . wow . . .

Each as beautiful as the last in her own way, each embodies the delicious glamour of Algiers.

Are they Algerian?

He drifts to the left of the lobby, not knowing which way to turn. Bill's being hailed from all sides; he manages all three sections of the club. He spots Moussa and quickly puts him in the picture. He can go to the dressing room or to the jazz club until he's on. He's entitled to two free drinks, after that he's on his own. Then Bill rushes off, swept away by a crowd of guests.

No way to open the door to the Oriental club, jammed with people. Music full blast, belly dancer on the floor, they're showering her with banknotes.

Moussa and Djelloul try the jazz club. As soon as they're inside the door, whew, they can breathe. Art Déco style, sensual lighting, it's like being in a private club in New York.

Onstage, the band. Bossa nova, smooth. Hey, it's Sam and Farid! Friendly winks.

Moussa and Djelloul prop up the bar. It's pleasantly cool, a/c, the sweet smell of class. Not too crowded, about ten of the tables are occupied, a few regulars at the bar. The women are stunning . . .

Music lovers, the audience appreciates the band, applauding after each number. Bill bursts in, races over to the sound booth, gets up onstage and murmurs something in Farid's ear, winks at Moussa, then exits and dives into the Oriental club.

Moussa explains to the barman, new artists, drinks . . . The barman knows the score. Two whiskeys, that'll get you going.

Onstage, Farid launches into a blues number, wringing tears from his guitar. Amazing, anyone would think he was American.

Moussa unwinds, reassures Djelloul. His eyes are everywhere. Get used to the interzone. Signature tune, break, the musicians gather at the bar while video monitors show jazz concerts.

Farid and Sam join Moussa, followed by Karim the percussionist and Yousef the bass player. They talk music, soften the fourth, emphasize the thirteenth. Sam's put on a bit of weight, he boxes Moussa affectionately. They're all happy for him, it's going to be great here. Rachid's coming later.

Half past midnight. Have a look around, the dressing rooms, get ready, onstage in fifteen minutes.

Moussa elbows his way through to the spacious dressing rooms—mirrors, chairs, fifteen or so people, dancers, musicians, groupies.

Mahmoud Aziz, the doyen, makes him welcome, introduces him to everyone. Someone gives Moussa a drink. He recognizes a few faces: Cheb Khaled pops his head around the door, he's on in a bit.

Yeah, the big guys, musicians from the TV. Nearly all the singers, male and female, are well-known stars. Already released records, cassettes.

The whiskey flows freely. Everyone's immaculate, bow ties, shiny shoes. Abdallah the foppish bass player is playing a game of poker with Nourdine-Chameau, the guitarist, 500 dinars a hand. And there's Abdelkader Chaou, the great chaâbi singer. Is that orange juice he's drinking?

Five minutes to go, and it's yours truly. The big moment. The musicians go on first, Moussa collects himself. He's really going to let them have it.

The band starts the intro, the host announces him,

and Moussa Massy pushes through the crowd to the stage amid a storm of applause.

Paralyzed with stage fright, he picks up the mike, blinking under the glare, not used to this. They repeat the intro and he's away. The PA's amazing, he can hear himself very clearly through the monitors. The band sounds like a Rolls Royce—intelligent, finesse, timing, volume, it's all perfect. Moussa really takes off with the second number, a reggae version of "Avava Inouva" by Idir, the way they rehearsed that afternoon.

Backed by the pulse of the double bass, Moussa gives his husky voice free rein. He's rocking now. People are starting to get up and dance, others sit and watch, new singer, check him out.

Third song, "Ayadho," by Rabah Asma. Mahmoud Aziz creates a wind effect on the synth, Moussa's flying. Tapping time with his foot, the chorus. The crowd on the floor goes crazy, the girls are mesmerized, a guy just stuffed a 200-dinar note down his shirt collar.

Straight for the killer blow, "Way Thelha" by Takfarinas. Moussa goes completely over the top, he dances with the mike stand, falls to his knees on the chorus, gets the audience to clap their hands, and fires up the band.

Moussa's going wild, it's the sixth time he's repeated the chorus. Mahmoud Aziz, the old rascal, winks at him every time. Go on, once more!

As the song ends to thunderous applause and ululations, singers even coming out of the dressing rooms to see, shit yeah, this kid's not bad. What's his name again? Massy Moussa? Pretty damn hot!

Bill's crouched in a corner, notepad in hand. He gives Moussa the thumbs-up.

Calm them down, "Hula Hoop" by El Hasnaoui, a gentle calypso that rises and falls. The double bass sways, Moussa feels the taste of coconuts on his tongue, the '50s, yeah, man . . . His voice is full, round, it fills the room through the speakers, ethereal and confident.

Two-hundred dinar notes rain down, tips. Afterwards, they get divided equally between the musicians and the DJ, he's entitled to a share. As the notes flutter down, you can bet they're all counting in their heads as they play.

One customer gives Moussa a princely 2,000 dinars to sing "Zwits Erwits."

The second he sees the two grand, Mahmoud Aziz launches into the intro. Moussa comes in with the song, an aggressive, alternative Berber hymn. Women knot scarves around their hips and dance, Kabyle style.

Moussa ups the tempo, improvises variations, exploring the whole range, stirs the crowd to a frenzy. They repeat the chorus for the tenth time, notes rain down, littering the stage.

It's over. Moussa comes off, exhausted. People congratulate him, everything's blurred, breathe, the dressing room. The host announces the great illusionist Bouras and his charming assistant, Nadia, the one every club regular's already . . .

In the dressing room, a sip of water, quick wash, naked dancers getting dressed, daily grind. Bill bursts in, pen between his teeth.

He quickly congratulates Moussa, then turns to the

female singer from Constantine. You're on next, Amel, just after Bouras, OK? Then he's gone.

Moussa relaxes, the place is packed, buzzing with people. Get me a drink, a drink, a drink. At least two hundred bottles of whiskey a night for the three clubs.

Hey, Djelloul! He'd vanished, gone off to hang out, drink, chat. Djelloul passes him the end of a spliff. Moussa lights it. He feels better, calm, relaxation of the gods. Hey, this is the life.

Nearly 3 a.m., time for a change of scene, come on, let's check out the jazz club or go to the disco. They leave the Oriental club bursting at the seams. The disco's just there, come on, let's go.

The minute the disco door opens, the pounding beat hits you in the pit of the stomach. The lights do the rest—magic, it's bewitching, glamour, glamour.

Chic clientele, rich kids, the sons of generals and oh-so-cool, stylish girls, *Algerian Graffiti*. The music—chart hits, good DJ, Samir, great patter, good vibe.

Second drink, Moussa and Djelloul go to the bar. Hey look, the barman's the immigrant from this afternoon. Hi! Moussa orders two whiskeys. The barman fills them to the brim, wink, cool, cheers, ice cubes clink in the glasses. Perched on his stool, Moussa gazes, stares, ogles, the looks, the faces, the comings and goings.

Bill appears. He's amazing:

"So, Massy? You know what? I think we should call you just Massy. It's easier and it sounds American. Know what I mean?"

Moussa, eyes shining:

"Ten out of ten. I was thinking the same thing. OK, I'll check with Rachid. He knows you, I think?"

Bill:

"Rachid? Oh yeah, good guy, I like his work. Have to change the poster outside. Sorry, got to run. It's the break in the jazz club. Have a couple of drinks on me."

Tactile and quick off the mark, Bill's off, sucked into the crowd. Moussa's glad to know him, he's a really solid guy.

Yes, just plain MASSY. Finished, all change, had enough of Moussa Massy.

It's true, MASSY is . . . cool, silky, Parisian, American, yeah. Bye-bye Moussa, hello MASSY.

Even Djelloul signals his approval, raising his glass refilled to the brim.

Moussa grabs his drink. Yeah, you see, this is where it all starts. The story of a singer on the brink of success. Yeah, success!

Moussa bursts out laughing. Shit, is this for real?

Le Triangle: he's at Le Triangle. The star of modern Kabyle music! Do a new poster, just put MASSY, in big letters, maybe red, sort it out with Rachid.

Speak of the devil, here he is. Rachid. African hat, baggy white pants, with Lynd', looks like . . .

They hug. Rachid had been huddled at the back of the Oriental. Saw the whole gig, Moussa's singing, his triumph. They discuss the MASSY business. Get rid of Moussa.

Rachid thinks it's a good idea. He'd been thinking that, too. MASSY's more media savvy, more direct. OK, re-do the poster, two days' work, MASSY in blue.

No, why not red, it's more in-your-face, more sensual. Rachid gives in, OK, but have to revamp the whole thing, the entire concept . . . But it can be done, no problem.

Rachid suggests winding up the night in the jazz club, he's got half a bottle of Scotch in there. They all get up, change of scene. Near the sound booth, Rachid's table, the best spot, behind the speakers.

Onstage, the band breaks into a very fast swing, syncopated rhythms. Moussa admires the musicians' skill, Farid on guitar, Sam on percussion, Mustapha on keyboard, and Yousef on bass.

Chilled atmosphere, air-conditioning on max, everything's just right.

Djelloul, Moussa, Rachid, and Lynd' toast Moussa's success.

Then everyone starts jamming—Malek on piano, Ahmed picks up the bass, Mourad on drums, Hocine on guitar, a different lineup. The next piece, it's Bill himself on guitar, with Arezki on drums, the other Farid on bass. Good bass player, Farid.

At the end of the jam, Bill introduces Mahfoud, the famous singer from Les Algiers. He comes onstage and sings "My Way" to a massive ovation.

Musicians take the stage on and off, nonstop. They're all excellent, the cream of Algiers. Respect, Moussa, for music, respect. His ears are wide open, he's learning.

Moussa's completely out of it. He gazes at the black-and-white poster of Billie Holiday behind the bar. He feels as if she's smiling at him alone, as if she knew that . . .

He still can't get over it: Le Triangle . . .

In the doorway . . . gorgeous black eyes, a mouth crying out to be ravaged with kisses. Hang on, that's Wahiba, the Méziani girl, isn't it?

Oh wow, look at that ass. She waves at him. Moussa gets up and walks over to her, Djelloul doesn't miss a thing.

Moussa has to lean close to hear her, because of the music. His nose brushing her perfumed breasts, he listens. She saw him sing just now, she thinks he's amazing. Her words interspersed with steamy looks, ripples of laughter. Wahiba is honey-tanned, cheeks like plump oranges, pure Arab thoroughbred.

Moussa instantly gets an erection. His reason falters, the Scotch, the spliff. He's got a hard-on, he wants Wahiba now. And she's there, open, moist . . . Go for it, for fuck's sake!

Asking for a light, Wahiba teases:

"You see, I need a match. I'm like a cigarette, I need a light to make me come alive."

Moussa, direct:

"Yes, but . . . where?"

Clinging to him, mischievous woman, spinning her web:

"You came with Djelloul, right? And the car's in the parking lot, isn't it?"

Moussa's even more aroused. The parking lot, of course. He goes over to Djelloul, car keys, got to sort something out, two minutes. Rachid smiles, Moussa knows he gets it, even Djelloul cottons on. But he's something else.

Dangling the keys, followed by Wahiba, Moussa heads for the parking lot, with his stiff cock. Says hi to the bouncer on the way out.

The minute they're in the car, Moussa leaps on top of Wahiba, kissing her all over.

The shadow of Fatiha's eyes hovers over him reproachfully. But no, it's different, this is pure lust. It bothers Moussa, all the same.

Wahiba relaxes him. Sinuous, she goes down on him, opens his zipper and sucks him very slowly. Shit, is this happening? Yes, it is, this is . . . God.

No, bullshitting, this is it! At last, I've found God.

Wahiba runs her tongue over the very pink tip of his cock, then takes it in her mouth up to the hilt. He stops her, raises her from behind and thrusts his cock inside her. She moans that she's coming, shouting "easy, brother," in Arabic. Moussa comes too, moaning loudly in Kabyle. Wahiba caresses and soothes him, he feels good.

Back to Le Triangle, no one any the wiser. Ciao, see you around. Moussa joins Rachid and the others. Nearly 5 a.m. One last drink, he's wrecked, yeah, completely wrecked.

Good crowd, all the musicians, B. B. King's singing on the screens. Around 5:30, closing time, meet up at the Terminus.

They all congregate there at the end of the night.

It's near the long-distance bus station, Algiers-Constantine, Algiers-Oran.

Everyone knows the café never closes. Twenty or so stray travelers sleeping with their heads on the tables, waiting for the first buses. Pale-faced soldiers on leave, country boys going back to their villages. Missed the boat in Algiers, barefoot, ragtag, with just enough money for the return ticket.

When the club crowd arrive, they cause a commotion. Clouds of aftershave and alcohol, tuxedos askew, ragged ties, dancers with their makeup smudged. Twelve cheese sandwiches, six chicken, twenty-two coffees with cream and seven lemonades.

From the terrace, you can see the port of Algiers with its warehouses and docks. In the background the curve of the bay, the beautiful, clear, famous Bay of Algiers.

The city wakes up, yawning. People already at work, the first traffic jams, streets coming to life. Moussa finishes his second cheese sandwich, laughing at one of Sam's jokes. Eight-thirty, ciao, everyone's leaving. Pay the bill, see you tonight, bye.

Moussa goes back with Djelloul, the sun's already very hot, it's going to be a scorching day, already August, time flies . . .

Djelloul drops Moussa outside his apartment building, garbage, flies, heat, Islamists already on sentry duty at the foot of the stairs.

Moussa puts on his shades, shut it all out. He slinks in, climbs the stairs, and crawls into bed.

Three

And so the summer goes on. Every night at Le Triangle, every Saturday at the beach with Djelloul. Sometimes he takes Maya and Fella with him. His older sisters won't come, they're too self-conscious. Their loss.

At Le Triangle, everything's just dandy now. Moussa's a hit and life's a breeze. Loads of dough, aftershave, silk shirts, ultra-hip catwalk shows, jazz concerts at the Ibn Zeydoun hall.

Moussa's a familiar figure in the most expensive restaurants of Ryadh El Feth—as befits someone in his position. Goldfish bowl. Hi, yeah, it's me. Starting to know people, real top-drawer, classy, government circles, serious money, power and influence.

Djelloul even told him that at this rate, he'll have a place to live in no time. Shh, shh, said Moussa, wait a bit.

Last week, a journalist did an excellent full-page piece on him in the *Nouvel Hebdo*. Serious article: "nothing like Takfarinas." Proper journalists at last!

August. At least 104 degrees in the shade. Cité Mer et Soleil's an oven—water cut off, garbage, kids, cockroaches, shortages of everything, Islamists crawling, going up the wall.

Moussa closes his heart, inoculates his senses. Nothing gets to him anymore, they can all go fuck themselves.

Got it?

One evening, Moussa's looking for his little Elvis Presley mirror. Algerian TV blasting from the living room.

Hunting for his mirror, Moussa listens to the news with half an ear. *"Saddam Hussein has invaded Kuwait . . . preparations for action . . . the West is violently opposed . . ."* What the hell's going on?

This reeks of world war, nuclear threat, the beards are in a frenzy. Meetings, marches, hmmm . . . it all stinks.

Having found his mirror, he shuts his ears and eyes. Doesn't want to know. Just wants to get on.

Moussa's made a lot of contacts since he's been at Le Triangle. Bill even introduced him to the governor of Ryadh El Feth, Colonel Denoudi, a cultured man, very distinguished.

There's always a crowd at the Colonel's table—powerful people, gorgeous women, showbiz types . . . Cheb Khaled, Djamal Allam, Safy Boutella. And they all congratulated Moussa, got to admit.

One afternoon, Moussa takes Fatiha to visit Ryadh El Feth and show her Le Triangle. He explains the equipment to her, the way the lights work. Fatiha's thrilled.

In the lobby, he kisses her surreptitiously on the neck. She protests, her cheeks flushed:

"Are you crazy, Méziane? Suppose someone sees us! Are you mad?"

Moussa loves going mad.

As they leave Le Triangle, they bump into Bill and his chick, Yasmine, a beautiful brunette, face of a dreamy sheep. Works in radio, French network.

Bill invites them for a drink on the terrace of the Épi d'Or. Abdallah the bass player arrives and joins them, yawning. Didn't get much shut-eye.

He chats to Moussa, can't get the words out. Some producer, a guy from Bab El Oued, interested in Moussa, wants to meet. But have to wait till September, he's in Spain right now. Abdallah gives him the producer's phone number, ordering another large coffee.

Producer?

Moussa silently quivers with excitement. Yasmine and Bill raise their glasses. Congratulations!

The icing on the cake, just what he needs. His eyes half closed, staring into space, softly caressing Fatiha's hair.

Moussa the lion takes a deep breath.

No, it's not enough, not yet. When you get to sing in front of forty thousand people, then you can say . . .

And anyway, it's all happening somewhere else—Europe, the USA. Now that's real class, when you see your mug everywhere—on TV and T-shirts and stuff. When you do videos, then you can really say, hey, I've made it.

But still, deep down, Moussa's pretty happy.

◆

September arrives, first fallen leaves, it's still very hot, and the beaches are packed. Those in the know go to the creeks.

All over the country, teachers, garbage collectors, and dockers are out on strike. Islamism's suffocating everything.

Abassi Madani and Ali Benhadj are on TV every day. It's the end of the world, an Islamic state looms.

Late September. Moussa decides to call the producer. His name's Lahbib. Meeting in Bab El Oued at 6 p.m.

Djelloul drives him there in a Renault 4L and drops him in Port-Saïd square. Throughout the journey, the engine splutters and there's a strong smell of gas. Needs a new crankshaft. Should be able to pick one up on the black market in Saint-Eugène.

Moussa walks along the seafront, the great Ketchaoua mosque at the end, on his right. He turns left and heads for the suburbs. Bab Azoun, streets with arcades, porches with caryatids.

Place des Martyrs, the lower Kasbah. He comes out by what used to be the Café Malakoff, postwar Algiers's Cotton Club. Sheer curiosity prompts him to wander over and take a look. There's still an old sign: "Café Hôtel Restaurant du Duc de Malakoff." What must that have been like . . . beautiful women with parasols, gentlemen in top hats and tails . . .

And now, breeze block, lemonade, flies, ruins . . .

Quickening his step, he reaches Bab El Oued. Incredible how it's changed. Garbage, kids, beards, kamis, like everywhere else in Algeria, the standard national formula.

Behind the Trois Horloges, Moussa looks for a cassette store, Pacific Editions. Lahbib produces most of today's big hits—rai, Kabyle, you name it. Please let it work.

The store assistant tells him that Lahbib's in the corner café. Moussa heads there, picking his way through the garbage, kids rummaging. Gandouras, beards, kamis, flip-flops.

The Essounna mosque just behind relays verses from the Koran through crackly loudspeakers.

Gloomy café, flies on lidless plastic sugar bowls. Torn old poster, soccer team, the famous national team of the old days, glory boys, '82 World Cup, Merzekane, Assad, Madjer, Belloumi, 2-1 v. Germany.

The waiter points out Lahbib, sitting with his back to Moussa at a table with two vaguely Islamist guys. Cloying heat. Lahbib's short, pudgy, and bald with a thick mustache. He's wearing a short-sleeved shirt, open at the neck to show off a fat gold chain.

He recognizes Moussa and waves him over to his table.

Lahbib's wearing flip-flops and is picking dirt from the toenails on his left foot:

"How're you doing? Abdallah must have spoken to you. I saw you sing at Le Triangle once. What a voice my friend, what a voice! Don't you worry, Lahbib's going to look after you. You have a great career ahead of you. It'll be a breeze."

The two guys get up, time for prayers. Moving on to the right foot, Lahbib:

"It'll be a piece of cake, I know it. With your voice . . . Tell me, do you compose? Have you got any lyrics, your own stuff?"

Moussa, apologetic:

"No, but . . ."

Lahbib, sniffing his chubby fingers:

"Don't worry, Uncle Lahbib'll find you a composer, a lyricist, an arranger, and it'll all be sorted. Five thousand copies to start with, to test the water, after that, we'll see, OK?"

Moussa tries to set out his strategy: Miles Davis, Prince, etc., but Lahbib's never heard of Prince, or anyone else . . .

". . . I mean something different . . ."

Lahbib:

"Oh you're a real worrier, you are, my friend! Trust me, I've got an ear for these things. Listen, I'll see you Friday at the Tarki brothers' studio. You'll record a guide vocal and then let the pros get on with it. Within a month you'll be in the *Local Rock* charts."

The flagship radio program *Local Rock,* barometer of the Algerian music scene. Charts, new Algerian music, Madonna in Arabic, reggae in Kabyle. Moussa often listens in, like everyone in the business, keeps his finger on the pulse. Of course, he's always dreamed of being on the charts . . .

Lahbib bums a cigarette from him:

"OK, so it's a deal? Relax, you've got a good voice, good face, that's all that matters . . ."

At the bar, the waiter's trying to tune into a station on the sputtering radio.

Moussa puts his finger in one ear:

"The thing is . . . I just wanted . . . not like everyone else . . ."

Lahbib, scratching his belly:

"What, you don't trust me?"

The waiter finds his station. Egyptian singer, Farid El Atrache? Abdelhalim Hafez?

You can't tell, radio's so crackly.

Moussa protests:

"With respect. I mean, I know you're very well-known in the business, Lahbib. I'm sorry. I'm not sure how these things work. Of course I trust you, but I want to do quality work . . ."

Stirring sugar into his coffee with his lighter, Lahbib:

"That's my department. You sing, then you let Lahbib's golden fingers take over the controls, OK? Everything will be fine, kiddo . . ."

"And for the title, I thought of '*Zombretto*,' it's . . ."

"Ah yes, why not? *Zombretto*? You are a funny one. Stop fretting, will you? Just leave it all to Lahbib."

Not completely reassured, Moussa returns to Cité Mer et Soleil, his head filled with dreams. Just as he arrives, a car honks. It's Djelloul. Moussa gets in. Djelloul munches a sandwich as he drives. Checking his appearance in his little Elvis mirror, Moussa tells him the news: producer, recording session, Friday, studio, *Local Rock*. Djelloul stops chewing and lets out a whoop. Shit man, this is it, you've made it!

Back home, he calls Rachid, tells him the deal. At once, Rachid suggests a game plan: session work with the best musicians in Algiers, work on the arrangements, mixing, hone the lyrics, the cover, take care of all the details. And the posters, decide where to put them up, add a banner: "New album: *Zombretto.*" Even if it's the first, people don't know.

That's 100 percent Rachid.

Moussa hangs up and capers around excitedly. He picks up Maya and throws her up in the air. Grandma, passing in the corridor, looks on disapprovingly. It's not natural to get so worked up.

The same thrill as in soccer, twenty years ago, when I was taken on for premier league NA Hussein-Dey's 15 to 17's team, fully-fledged center forward. Yes, same moist, radiant feeling of joy filled with smells of other places, other times. My first official match, proper soccer cleats, blue-and-white-striped socks, blue shorts, blue-and-white shirt, with number 10 on the back.

Z'hor had ironed everything the evening before, hadn't slept a wink all night. At dawn, Mohand took me to the club, the managers, the players, the supporters, the bus engine running. It was at the El Annasser stadium, against Algiers's dreaded Mouloudia team. I scored a goal, the only one of the match. The coach ran around the stadium with me sitting on his shoulders, the supporters cheered.

Over the next few days, Moussa and Rachid carry out the plan, putting up the posters themselves with Scotch tape and scissors. Everywhere—on walls, in the windows of cassette stores and bookstores, in tea rooms, at the fine arts school. More than four hundred posters in total.

Moussa tells his friends and the musicians at Le Triangle the news. Everyone's happy for him. Well done, Moussa, you're on your way! A round of drinks to celebrate!

Long discussion with Bill. Tips: phase inversion, be careful, always do the mix early in the morning, no drink or drugs, don't fuck up.

When it's time for his set, Moussa bounds onto the stage, a Berber leopard. He leaps about, lights, music, life. The crowd's electrified, Moussa MASSY slays 'em. He repeats the chorus for the fifteenth time, I'll show them, they'll be on their knees.

Leaning against the bar, Bill nods approvingly. Looking him in the eyes, Moussa goes wild. This is what you call a triumph!

◆

A few days later, Moussa's invited to a private showing at the Frantz Fanon gallery in Ryadh El Feth. The painter Ferhat's beginning to make a name for himself, articles in the papers, TV programs.

Moussa tells himself he'll never be on Algerian TV for the simple reason that he doesn't speak Arabic.

At least not the stiff Arabic of the Koran—official, stilted, foreign to his culture.

Street Arabic, no problem, Moussa plays with it—chaâbi music, the Kasbah, working-class districts, he's in his element.

But the Arabic of the TV, of the ruling classes, is not the same. As far removed as low Latin from modern-day French. No kidding.

Nearly 4 p.m., the gallery's packed with intellectuals, artists, critics, loads of babes.

It's good. Civilization is when guys and chicks can mingle, simply, without too much . . .

Moussa recognizes a few faces. Ferhat comes over and introduces him to some guys from RCD, a brand-new political party. Moussa likes them. Especially the leader, Saïd Saadi, he's for real.

There's a Berber feel to the place with an exhibition of Berber jewelry and books on at the same time. And even Colonel Denoudi's here with his fluttering entourage.

Moussa goes around the paintings and is soon bored to tears. Doesn't get it at all. Abstract paintings aren't his thing, he prefers landscapes, modern posters and stuff.

Ferhat drags him off to Yoyo's next door for a drink with a couple of friends, Aomar and Mokrane. They're university lecturers, leftie Berberists.

The drinks are on Ferhat, four beers:

"Cheers!"

Mokrane raises his beer mug:

"To our age-old civilization, repressed by Arab imperialism!"

Wow, they're getting right in there. Moussa concentrates on his beer.

Mokrane continues:

"Yeah, we're the Sioux of Algeria, the Kurds of the Maghreb, the Irish of the Arab world, cooped up and deprived of our culture. Fuck it, when you think that us Berbers were here before anyone else . . ."

That's true, Moussa silently agrees.

Ferhat puts things in perspective:

"Yeah, but still, you can't be too strict, there are geostrategic truths."

"What? Who's being too strict? They are, the Arabs! They're the ones who say: strictly forbidden. They should just give us back our land, our ancestors' blood . . ."

"I don't agree with you there. I'm pro secession. Too much has gone into the pot."

"Yes, but there are degrees, without going as far as secession. There's regionalization, federalization, look at Switzerland, the USA . . ."

Aomar knocking back his drink:

"Well, I'm for secession! Don't want anything to do with that Arab scum. They're shit . . ."

Ferhat:

"Now that's racism . . ."

Mokrane:

"What? Hang on, hang on. Look me in the eyes, Ferhat, and tell me honestly, in a word, whether you have anything in common with an Arab. With an Islamist?"

"When you put it like that, it's . . . but there's history. And besides, we're Algerians first and foremost, yes or no?"

Aomar, an olive poised between finger and thumb:

"Don't confuse the issue. It's true, we're Algerians, that's not the point. But what does it actually mean to be Algerian, or Arab? Well then, no! Because nobody, not Ben Bella, Boumedienne, or Chadli has recognized that the Berbers are the exception and that's fundamental to the national character. Nobody!"

Mokrane, the stickler:

"Algeria is an Arab-Muslim nation, it's in the fucking constitution, right? They've all negated Berber culture. For them, it's just a little local dialect, crafts, folklore. What's your view, brother?"

All eyes on Moussa:

"Er . . . as far as music goes, I don't think there are too many problems, but . . ."

Ferhat:

"He's right. In fact, it's thanks to music that the Berber cause has been heard all over the world. Thanks mostly to Idir."

They all agree, yes, thanks to Idir, in the 1970s.

Mokrane fumes:

"They threw us in prison every time we said: look at us. So now we're going to help ourselves. We'll circulate images of the great Berbers, Saint Augustine, Septimus Severus, Apuleus . . ."

Ferhat, pointing to Moussa:

"and Massinissa . . ."

Moussa blushes with pleasure. Aomar places his hand on his shoulder:

"Ah yes, MASSY, that's some name, it's like a shield, you know. Culture's all we have left . . . we're relying on you artists. You're our most fertile ground."

Moussa feels entrusted with a heavy load. It's true he's a Berber, but not . . . a Berberist, because politics . . . Don't get too involved. It reminds him of what happened to Sahnoun. That's how he ended up autistic.

But ultimately, they're right. Why do the Kabyles always get crushed . . . ?

◆

One Friday afternoon, Djelloul drops Moussa in Kouba, at the Tarki brothers' studio in the garage of an enormous villa. Lahbib's there, with the two brothers. They're mixing a rai number Lahbib's producing.

Moussa settles down in a corner to watch them work. The equipment, synthesizers, flashing lights. When you get into a studio, it's a whole new ball game. A new chapter, the acid test. You multiply yourself, mass audience.

Ten minutes later, it's Moussa's turn. Lahbib pulls out two songs scribbled in an old spiral-bound notebook. One of the Tarki brothers hums the tune for him, strumming along on the guitar.

Moussa isn't too keen, it sounds a bit cheesy. Not at all what he'd had . . .

Lahbib schmoozes him, don't worry, just wait till it's been mixed, you won't recognize your own voice, reverb, effects. The Tarki brothers echo his words. But Moussa's defiant, he insists on doing one of his own songs, his own reggae version of Idir's "Avava Inouva." It's new, no one's done it before.

They give in. OK, why not? Got to admit it, it's new.

Let's try the vocal, cans, they give him a beat, Moussa tries to pitch his voice, unaccompanied.

Lahbib:

"All seven songs in two hours, that's all the time we've got, handsome."

Moussa refuses, takes off the headphones, wants to work on the song alone for a bit, learn the lyrics, the melodies. Seven songs in two hours, are you crazy or what?

Lahbib fumes:

"Listen, are you trying to put one over on me? I booked the studio for you, it costs a ton!"

One of the Tarki brothers calms him down:

"Drop it, Lahbib, he's right. I'll record the melodies on a cassette for him and tomorrow we'll start again. No extra cost, I promise. We'll foot the bill."

Lahbib thanks them, so does Moussa. Shit, that was close!

Be here tomorrow, same time.

Cassette in his pocket, Moussa flies home, his heart has wings. He bounds up the stairs to the amazement of the gawping brats.

Singing inside his head, he goes into his bedroom. Sahnoun's still absorbed in his SAS.

Today Le Triangle's closed. Moussa picks up his mandola, his Walkman, and some spliff, and goes out to the back of the building, looking over the bay. Behind him, the garbage bins.

All night, spliffs, rewind, count time, learn the tunes, the lyrics. It's very basic. He tries to embellish, find variations, give the thing some substance. After three hours' work, it's all beginning to come together, to have some meat.

He goes over the seven songs one after the other, one leading into the next, as if he were in the studio.

Enjoying himself, he even finds ways to link them. He's bursting with ideas, strokes of inspiration. He'll suggest them, persuade Lahbib and company.

The night's pregnant with stars. Facing the water, Moussa can taste the tang of the sea. He turns around. Some twenty garbage-bin kids, young dropouts are sitting in a circle around him, their eyes shining in the dark.

They've been listening to Moussa all evening, while he was yowling with his headphones on.

Spartacus—beard, kamis—stands up and claps. He shyly requests a song, "El Herraz" by Guerrouabi. Fire in his soul, Moussa launches into the ancient Algiers ballad, redolent of jasmine and enchantment, magic and beautiful damsels.

Brings back the good old days, the '60s in black and white, the Algerian War of Independence, inter-high school soccer matches, the first stirrings of love at fifteen, daughters of French peace corps volunteers, blonde, freckled, in the hot Ramadan nights, mint and cumin. Ah, the good old days.

That reminds me of Mouloud, my big brother, killed in action, he must have been around eighteen then, the best age. I bet he had a good time, goddammit, I bet, with the Vespas, parties with the *pieds-noirs,* eating prawns at Fort-de-l'Eau, coming back from the beach, drinking anisette on the terrace of Le Coq Hardi.

All that's gone now. I've seen photos of him at the time, a right Don Juan with his white shoes, hip-hugging pants, thin mustache, and greased-back hair. I bet he blew them away at dances—the orange festival at Boufarik, the cherry festival in Miliana.

No more oranges now, no more cherries.

Algeria's suffering a scourge these days, something's been ruined forever.

Sighing, Moussa gets up, despite protests from his audience. He walks away, waving good-bye with his mandola.

His heart full of sweet nostalgia, he creeps up to his apartment and falls asleep, his head full of the '60s.

◆

The next day, same time, he's at the Tarki brothers' studio. Lahbib's there, red nose, seems to have a bad cold. Greetings, a coffee, Moussa chats, and Lahbib sneezes all over his shirt:

"Sorry, I've got a stinking cold. Slept with no pajama top last night, there were drafts."

Moussa wipes his shirt:

"No problem. Right, can we start?"

The Tarki brothers set up the equipment, test the mike, fine, let's go.

Beat in the headphones, Moussa pitches his voice, OK, let's go, metronome, two-bar intro.

Apart from the first song, he finishes all of them, one after the other, in one take. He even slips in a few variations he worked on the night before.

When he's done, they're amazed. One of the Tarki brothers:

"Bravo! In one take—I've hardly ever seen that. You're going places, man!"

Between two sneezes, Lahbib rubs his hands and cadges a cigarette from Moussa:

"There you are. In a week it'll be sorted. I knew it, the minute I heard you sing. You'll be the biggest star in Algeria. Right, now you've recorded your voice, let us take care of the rest. I'll call you when it's all in the can."

What about the musicians, who will they be? I know guys who . . .

Lahbib, affably:

"Don't worry, I tell you. Oh, you're a pain, you are! Listen, as soon as the master's ready, we'll listen to it together and if you don't like it, we'll change it, no problem. Does that suit you?"

Moussa furrows his brow, smiling:

"OK. But you know, if I say that, it's because I want the end product to be good, for all our sakes."

Lahbib pretends to agree, filching another cigarette. The Tarki brothers nod. OK, in theory at least. They rewind the tape.

Moussa ventures to raise the delicate matter of the contract. Lahbib blows his nose energetically and explodes:

"Hold your horses! This is the deal: 10,000 dinars straight fee for the initial release, then we share the royalties 50-50, OK?"

Moussa's at a loss, he tries to say that money's not the main thing, it's . . .

OK, ciao, he leaves the villa.

He hails a passing cab and goes home. A good deal, in spite of everything. Might be able to get some mileage out of this cassette, with Rachid and the others.

Taxi drops him outside Bouhar's. There's a long line of people buying bread. His head buzzing with sounds and colors, Moussa cuts through the line, steps over kids and puddles of piss. He makes his way to his staircase. The walls, graffiti palimpsests—*FIS, Love, Canada, Australia.*

On the stairs, Moussa can already hear Farid playing the guitar solos, Mustapha banging out the chords on the piano, Karim swinging expertly to a Charleston. The overall effect a cross between Miles Davis and Prince, something like that.

For the final mix, call in Bill if he's free. Yeah, Moussa has great ideas for that. He can already see the cover design, with Rachid fussing over the details as always, the grading, the layout, the printer. Massy a bit more to the right, there. Perfect! . . .

Moussa can also see Rachid organizing a press conference—posters, cassettes on stands with MASSY in giant letters, printed T-shirts. There's a guy who does a great job in El Harrach.

Good old Rachid.

Part Three

◆

One

For months now, a complicated financial scandal's been rocking the country. It's a sordid business involving money trafficking and embezzlement, the president's son is implicated.

Arrests were made in Ryadh El Feth, the center of an extensive network of corruption, with bosses led away in handcuffs.

They're all at each other's throats—the president's son, the boss of the Grill Room, executives from the Banque Extérieure d'Algérie, Ryadh El Feth authorities . . . 80 billion's said to have been siphoned off.

The scandal's headline news in all the papers. General outcry in Algiers, gas stations go on strike. The FIS has a field day, *Allah O Akbar,* postal workers and doctors join the strike. Divine justice. Air Algérie pilots strike, there are demos, the bakers strike, heads must roll. *Allah O Akbar,* the smell of gunpowder.

Of gunpowder and garbage.

As always, the Prime Minister plays the international conspiracy card: Israel, France, the CIA, Iran, like last time.

Moussa smiles: their paranoia's pathetic. They've got to be kidding. They're still harping on the same old theme after thirty years of the FLN. The whole world's permanently plotting against our noble and invincible country. Interstellar jealousy, we have proof, we'll produce it when the time is right.

They've got to be kidding . . .

The brand-new parties give the government a drubbing. The brand-new newspapers, too.

Officially, silence on the air waves. Hybrid rumor gains currency and reigns supreme: "Apparently the president's in league with the FIS."

The most absurd gossip spreads, there's talk of assassinations, a coup d'état, the Resistance movement. It's the sole topic of conversation in bars, mosques, barbers, and Turkish baths: 80 billion, president's son, FIS, civil war.

Moussa's suffocating. Stay on track, fight his corner.

There's a new régime in Ryadh El Feth. Colonel Denoudi was given the push months ago, replaced by an FLN administrator, a total killjoy. No more public entertainment, nothing.

Everything's gone gray. Color, beauty, and sophistication are banished. The FLN model regains its legendary place: purple hue, Libyan mustache, chewing tobacco, beret, burnous, gutteral "r"s.

There's been a change of management at Le Triangle, too. Notorious hoodlums, the new bosses soon make their slimy mark. The clientèle visibly deteriorates, bus-shelter whores and small-time crooks. Bill talks seriously about quitting.

The first brawls break out at Le Triangle. Moussa watches one of the new bosses head-butt a customer and knock him out, in front of everyone. Blood on the carpet, girls in evening dress screaming.

Nail-biting times. Moussa's increasingly anxious. One burning question obsesses him: Is this the end of the beginning or the beginning of the end?

At night, in his fourteen-to-three-rooms apartment, pressed against his wall, sleep eludes him.

◆

Moussa's been waiting for a call from Lahbib for two weeks now. Not a peep. I don't like this, what the hell's he up to?

One afternoon, around 5 p.m., Moussa bumps into Spartacus in the building:

"Congratulations, Moussa, I heard you on the radio yesterday. Bravo, you're a big star now!"

Moussa:

"What do you mean, on the radio? I was on the radio?"

Spartacus, smirking:

"Yes, yes, I heard you. They played your latest song on *Local Rock*. Listen this evening, around six, they're bound to play it again."

Mystified, Moussa races home and switches on the radio. *Local Rock* starts in five minutes.

Nerves raw, he pours himself a coffee, settles down in his room, and lights a cigarette.

Sahnoun's glued to his SAS.

Ryma, star DJ, introduces the program. Jingles, the

charts ". . . and at number 15, a new voice, MASSY . . . To vote, call . . ."

Stunned, Moussa hears himself singing on the radio. I don't believe it.

That motherfucker Lahbib!

Hard to recognize his voice, drowned out by a load of echo, drum machine, sounds mechanical.

It's not true?

Tears in his eyes, he calls Rachid who's just heard the program. He consoles Moussa. Sue Lahbib, get a lawyer on his ass, go to the press.

Little stroll around the neighborhood, gauge the impact. A lot of people heard the program, they all think it's great. His sisters, Djelloul . . .

That evening at Le Triangle, too, some of the musicians listened to the radio, general verdict: pretty damn good.

But Moussa knows very well it's unspeakable shit.

The next day, he hotfoots it to Lahbib's cassette store in Bab El Oued. The young sales assistant, dragon shirt and Islamist goatee, tells him Lahbib's in the warehouse at the back of the store. Moussa finds Lahbib in a corner with three Islamists, counting out boxes of cassettes of the Koran, sermons by Ali Benhadj.

No scruples, Lahbib, business is business.

Calculator in hand, Lahbib spies Moussa:

"Ah, it's you! I was just about to call you. Haven't had a moment, got to do my taxes. But I've got one of your songs on *Local Rock,* they're playing it at the moment. Have you heard it? Not bad, eh?"

In front of the Islamists, Moussa:

"It's a pile of shit, you bastard!"

He goes for Lahbib. The Islamists calm him down, in the name of the Lord, Satan be cursed.

Lahbib, sweating profusely:

"Don't get mad, I only gave them one song. We haven't duped the cassettes yet. Just testing the water. Anyway, I wanted to see you. Look, here's an advance."

He struggles to extract a filthy wad of 1,000 dinar notes from his back pocket and hands it to Moussa.

Moussa takes it and demands a proper contract with a strict schedule of payments for the remainder. Stop fucking me around, OK? Lahbib says OK, he'll get to his lawyer and Moussa'll have the contract within a week.

"The album will have to be mixed again, it's crap. I'm bringing in my own musicians, my engineer. Redo the whole thing, there's no way you can release it like that."

Lahbib wipes his sticky hands on his shirt and pacifies him:

"Yeah, no sweat, we'll do it the way you want. Calm down! You're such a pain in the ass!"

Moussa leaves and wanders around Bab El Oued. It's like Kabul, Peshawar, the third world as shown on TV. It's madness . . .

What the hell happened to the real Bab El Oued? The real fucking street kids? The true grit of Algiers?

It's true, "all that remains of the oued is its stones." Fucked. The whole thing should be flattened, nothing can ever grow on this dunghill, that's for sure.

Below, El Kettani swimming pool, former haunt of the beautiful people of Algiers. Glorious tans, gleaming gold chains, the chicks' sensual smiles, floral bathing suits, limbs toasted to perfection. *You're tickling me, Razika, stop it!*

The minute spring arrived in all its glory, people would descend on El Kettani swimming pool. The school sports teacher brought the entire third-year class once a week. Diving boards, swan dives. The first girls, platonic yearning, suggestive eyelash fluttering, songs by Adamo, *Viens, viens, ma bruuuuunne,* orange sherbets.

◆

Meanwhile, Moussa continues to meet Fatiha in secret. They go for walks in the Bois des Arcades, meet in the tea rooms. Moussa's tired of hiding. He wants to talk to Fatiha's parents once and for all; can't go on like this.

One Thursday afternoon, he decides to call them and tell them he's coming to see them.

Suit and tie, model son-in-law, he arrives holding a box of cakes. His senses tingling, he slowly climbs the stairs. This is the best day of his life.

Third floor, he rings the bell. Fatiha's mother opens the door. Tight-lipped, veiled, and bespectacled, she invites him into the sitting room. On the way, she shoos the kids into another room.

Here, too, there must be a lot of them crowded into one apartment. Eight? Ten?

Fatiha's father arrives. Glasses, slippers, a retired Post Office worker. Moussa turns on the charm. The mother serves coffee and cakes. They chat about this and that, the family, the rising cost of living, shortages, politics.

Speaking in Kabyle, of course.

It's the first time Moussa's been to their place, to Fatiha's home, trailing her. His gaze roves around the room: stag-head barometer on the wall, a verse from the Koran above the front door, Post Office calendar on the fridge.

How many nights has he fantasized about Fatiha—imagining her daily routine, taking a bath, drying her hair on the balcony, doing her homework, cooking . . .

After a good half hour of preliminaries, Moussa finally blurts out his garbled request, wrapped in the appropriate rhetoric, proverbs, Kabyle sayings:

"I entreat your blessing, in the name of your family's good reputation which extends beyond Kabylia, the Land of Free Men, 'God bless the ignorant.' My ancestors bequeathed me a heart, arms, and a tongue. These are my land, and they are at your disposal. I ask you for the hand of Fatiha, your daughter. I will take the utmost care of her, I swear. I will soon have an apartment, I promise her a future filled with Good and Virtue, as God is my witness."

Oh, come off it! With a prim sidelong glance at her husband, Fatiha's mother:

"Um . . . , we have great esteem for you, Méziane. Your family's well thought of. But . . . we've already chosen a husband for our daughter Fatiha. She is to marry her cousin, an engineer. He has an apartment, a car, a good job. You must understand how hard it is for parents to safeguard their child's future these days."

Moussa can't believe his ears. He cuts short the conversation, rises politely to his feet, and takes his leave. He hurtles down the stairs. At the bottom, he aims a furious kick at the big garbage bin crawling with kids.

That evening at Le Triangle, things go badly onstage. Bum notes, out of time, Bill asks what's wrong. Moussa apologizes, feeling a bit rough, do better next time. As soon as he finishes, he dives into the jazz club to get blasted. Drink after drink, joint after joint.

At dawn, he goes straight back home. Forget about the Terminus.

Sobbing against his wall, he falls asleep consumed by Fatiha's immense green gaze, the smell of her neck, tormented by memories.

The next day, as soon as he opens his eyes, he phones Fatiha. To make sure she loves him . . . it's not true. After all this time . . . soon it'll be six years.

Her voice strained, Fatiha confirms:

"Um . . . yes, it's Larbi, a cousin. He's an agricultural engineer. It's my parents' decision, I have to . . . what else can I do?"

Moussa stammers:

"But . . . but . . . do . . . do . . . you love me or not, that's the question?"

"That's got nothing to do with it, it's my parents. Listen . . ."

He, biting his nails:

"What do you mean, nothing to do with it? It's got everything to do with it! You have to choose, it's your parents or me. You're an adult, for God's sake!"

Fatiha, dutiful daughter:

"You know very well I can't go against my parents. I think we'll have to . . . forget each other, Méziane, even though I love you . . ."

Moussa bangs the phone down, sobs bursting from his throat. The end, ciao. Women, all the same. Fucking bitches.

When Djelloul comes to pick him up, Moussa's already drunk, bootleg gin from Sid Ali, who works as a flight attendant. Pure reflex, he takes the joint Djelloul passes him and takes a long toke, his eyes dark and belligerent.

On the way, he confides in Djelloul, who's silently in love with Nacéra.

Djelloul tries to console him:

"Fuck it, forget her. There are plenty of women on this earth. Don't make yourself ill over it. Especially not for a bitch who strung you along for more than five years . . ."

No, he doesn't get it. Fatiha, garlands of memories, mottled ghosts dancing in his consciousness, the dusky fragrance of jasmine that kindles the memory and sets the body on fire.

No, doesn't get it. Can't explain.

Forget?

That evening, Moussa drinks and smokes all night, holed up in the jazz club sound booth with Djelloul and some of the musicians. Bill comes in to take a couple of drags. Hey, take it easy guys, don't screw up. OK, Bill.

Worse, Le Triangle's changed so much, gone downhill, turned into a pig sty full of losers. The glitterati don't come anymore. Bill's sick of it, every night he says it's his last, Yasmine, his broad, hasn't been in for ages.

Moussa stares fixedly at a customer at the bar. Shaggy hair, jogging top, shoes worn down at the back, like slippers, looks like a chicken-seller from the country. A few months ago, he'd never have dreamed of tramping all over the carpet of Le Triangle with his filthy feet, not in his wildest imaginings.

The evening wears on. Drinking, smoking, music. Fatiha's image tears him apart. His heart's clenched like a fist, tears burn his eyes. Abruptly he stands up and runs to the toilets where he double-locks the door.

There, he weeps softly over his life, his cancelled destiny. Wiping away his tears, he lights a cigarette and takes two long drags. Then, biting his lip, he jabs the red-hot tip into his forearm, making a deep burn.

◆

Lahbib hasn't called back yet about signing the contract— the slippery eel, he slides through your fingers and escapes. Moussa seethes like a volcano, especially since Fatiha left him. He's like a caged beast, no outlet for his anger, which rages more intense, more violent, each day.

One day, back from college, Nacéra comes and talks to him:

"Méziane, a girlfriend lent me your cassette. You didn't tell me you'd brought out a cassette."

Brought out a cassette?

Moussa snatches it from her. The sleeve's a real mess: "*Moussa MASSY: the new Takfarinas.*" Overlapping colors, blurred photo, he's barely recognizable. Dull, greenish background. Hideous . . .

He turns it over: Sonorama Editions, that's it, no title, no credits, no copyright, no nothing. He grabs his Walkman and plays the cassette.

Unbelievable! The sound is shit—songs cut before they're finished, distortion. Moussa wants to murder someone . . .

Telephone. Nacéra picks it up, call for Moussa. It's Lahbib. Good timing, I'll give him what for.

They both yell into the phone at the same time.

Lahbib explains that someone stole the master tape from the studio and pirated the cassette. But don't worry, I'll have 'em, lawyers and everything.

At the same time, Moussa yells that he's the one who's been had, bastard sonofabitch, and he'll have him all right.

Moussa slams down the phone. Nacéra comes running, urging him to calm down.

Taxi. Twenty minutes later, he's at Rachid's. He finds Rachid in a foul mood. He's fed up:

"Fucking country, shitty mentality! I don't know what to say, Moussa, I've had it up to here. Farid and Sam have legged it to Paris, Bill, too, with Yasmine. It stinks here, it's gonna blow. Can't you smell the sulfur in the air?"

Moussa downs vodka after vodka. Everything's mixed up in his mind, Fatiha leaving him, the FIS, fourteen-to-three-rooms, Lahbib.

He methodically chews what's left of his nails:

"Listen, Rachid, we're gonna try something else. I'm going to produce this cassette myself. Yeah, all my dough. We're going to do this fucking cassette the way we want to."

Rachid fiddles around with the CDs, pretending to tidy them. He seems to be trying to say something:

"Moussa, I think this is . . . more serious. Open your eyes. The country's fucked. The FIS is going to take power, that's for sure. There's nothing more to do here, even in my line of work. There's no paper or equipment, there's nothing, it's just not possible to work anymore. Lynd's already over there, in Paris."

"Really, on holiday?"

"No, Moussa, not on holiday, to live. We're quitting, it's finished. I'm going to join her at the end of the month."

Moussa, anxious:

"For . . . good?"

"For a good while, at least, I think. There's nothing left for us here, best to get out. You should think about it seriously, too. The shit's going to hit the fan in this country, Algeria's going mad."

Moussa digests the news. Kick in the balls, icy pain, total paralysis.

Rachid's leaving.

He feels a terrible void opening up inside him, as if night's suddenly fallen. If Rachid goes, then it's really over. Shut up shop, curtains. Move on.

His heart sinking, Moussa leaves Rachid's place. He's devastated. Only one desire, to drink, drink, drink.

He ends up in a seedy bar. Beer, beer, beer, chat, FIS, black market, civil war, emigration, contacts, visas, Canada, Australia, the ship's letting in water on all sides.

Rachid's leaving. Good night all, it's all well and truly over.

◆

Moussa didn't want to go to Rachid's farewell party. No, too painful, besides there'd be loads of people there, the in crowd. Been once before, not my scene, feel out of place. Always preferred seeing Rachid on my own, or in a small group, two or three of us, no more. Not the same buzz, too wound up all evening.

What's more, Rachid's going for good, so . . .

Massively shy, that's how Moussa is. He prefers to make a clean break. Change tack, follow your star. Good luck, take care.

The day of the party, Rachid drove over to Moussa's apartment building to fetch him, after hundreds of phone calls. Moussa lay on his stomach on the floor of Djelloul's car, hiding. Rachid never saw him.

Moussa didn't even want to read the note Rachid left. He threw it off the balcony and watched it flutter in the air and land in a puddle of piss below.

No heart left for anything, Moussa carries on at Le Triangle. He's on autopilot, one song leading into another. Not an ounce of feeling, nothing.

In any case, no one's listening. You can wail whatever you like, the customers are bootleggers, their pockets stuffed with easy bucks, wallowing in adulterated whiskey and the venom of old whores.

Bill finally left, Rachid, Farid, Sam . . . all the good guys have gone. Le Triangle's become really sordid—a grungy, shady dive.

Brawls every night, the place is a black-market haven, awash with loot and Scotch. A different breed. Look at it, just take a look. Something else is going down now.

A new mob, born of the garbage bins, vice and . . . God.

Moussa doesn't react anymore, shuts it all out. Everything's fucked—the lighting's down, only one side of the PA works, spotlights smashed, carpet in tatters, and no one gives a damn.

For the first time, Moussa drinks and smokes with the local guys, low life, fated never to move.

They're greatly honored, you can imagine: Moussa Massy, the star, deigning to . . .

They often hang out behind the apartment building, wasteland, garbage bins. They introduce him to 6.15 tabs, the speed of the slums, the young junkies' drug of choice.

6.15s diffract your senses. Exploding disjointed perceptions, shattered mirror, pure Picasso. It blows your mind, you're somewhere else.

Day after day, Moussa deteriorates, at the same pace as Algeria, *allegro*. Moussa concocts his mix of dope, alcohol, and 6.15s, every shitty day God gives shitty Algeria.

He even loses a front tooth. That's all he needs. At home, can't talk to anyone anymore, family autism, rage always on the brink of erupting.

Apache tactics, he skulks in corridors and on the stairs, avoids bumping into anyone, becomes totally transparent.

Clashes between FIS and law students. Four dead, killed with swords, Islamist commandos. Moussa, out of his head on 6.15s, doesn't give a shit. Let them kill each other, they can all fuck off . . .

Shortages, endless lines of people waiting for bread, milk, life. Processions of men, women, and children stretching to infinity, their hands reaching out for nothing.

Each week, the streets and public squares are invaded. FIS demos, hundreds of thousands of bearded kamis-wearers reciting the Koran, the glint of murder in their eyes.

Speaking in Arabic.

Democrats' counterdemos: ties, glasses, mustaches, feminists in jeans, cigarettes, and bullhorns.

Speaking in French.

✦

One November evening, when Moussa arrives at Le Triangle, the boss comes over and takes his arm. Let's have a little chat. He takes Moussa to the café next to the Grill Room opposite.

The usual opening gambits. Moussa listens without really hearing as the boss trots out "good singer . . .

but . . . you understand . . . new lineup . . . our customers . . . come back in six months, we'll see . . . last night tonight."

Then he leaves Moussa sitting there and vanishes back inside Le Triangle.

To put it bluntly, Moussa's fired, replaced by Mohand Akli, a fossil of Kabyle music, cutthroat shark from the coast.

High on alcohol and drugs, Moussa weeps onstage as he sings. But, like every other night, no one gives a shit. New customers, just like La Chésa's in fact, pimps, moron billionaires, gold-toothed whores.

The musicians have heard. They console Moussa, sympathetic thumps on the back, don't worry about it, they're all bastards!

Djelloul didn't come tonight, stomach upset.

Moussa takes refuge in the jazz club sound booth, smoking spliffs with the band.

The video's broken, one of the giant stage speakers has been out of action for the last three weeks, the lights on the glass ceiling have all been shattered, the carpet's black with grime. The bosses don't give a fuck. They just want to make as much dough as they can.

As fast as they can.

Five o'clock in the morning, smashed out of his skull, Moussa makes his way home on foot, under a fine drizzle.

Hair disheveled, plastered to his cheeks, sobbing and laughing hysterically at the same time, he can barely walk.

It's nearly light, a wan sun is pushing through the clouds. The cafés are opening up, workers in a hurry, first buses, cars, watch out, road's slippery.

Silk shirt billowing, alpaca pants flapping, green crocodile shoes, Moussa advances like a crab, clutching at walls, trees, and lampposts for support. He zigzags across the road robotically, drivers honk angrily.

Around 5:30 he reaches Hussein Dey, a swarm of Islamists are hurrying toward the mosque for dawn prayer.

There are a good hundred of them, moving in silence, zealous and sullen. The only sound is "phittt." Beards, kamis, flip-flops, phittt, beards, kamis, flip-flops, phittt . . .

Moussa has to push through the crowd to get to Brossette and walk up the slope to his apartment building on the left.

Soaked to the skin, his shirt unbuttoned to the navel, hair wet and sticky with gel, he walks like a zombie, reeking of alcohol and club fumes.

Moussa cuts through the crowd, kamis, beards, the smell of moldy tombs. He can feel their hate-filled stares, he knows what they're thinking, faggot and all that. But fuck 'em. He keeps going.

All eyes are on him, the Islamists spitting their contempt. A few shout insults. Some very young boys throw stones at him. One hits him on the forehead, he wipes it with his hand and sees blood.

Moussa turns around to face them, then, staring at them defiantly, he licks the blood from his hand and grabs his balls:

"You fuckers, suck my cock! Assholes! Up yours!"

Seven Islamists, adults this time, lay into him, punching, kicking, beating him with sticks.

An elderly Islamist steps in:

"Stop, this is not our aim! Leave him alone, you can see he's just a sad drunk. We must concentrate our Jihad on this ungodly government that scorns Islam and wallows in filth and corruption. We must cut off its head, cursed be Satan, *Allah O Akbar!*"

They chorus: *"Allah O Akbar,"* then leave Moussa slumped on the ground, unconscious.

Taking pity, the waiter from a neighboring café throws a bucket of water over Moussa's head.

A good quarter of an hour later, Moussa comes to, his head burning, a gash above his eye. With a weary movement, he tries to adjust his tattered silk shirt, which is now red with blood.

Staggering, still full of alcohol, ribs bruised, he limps on. Lost a crocodile-skin shoe in the fray.

Passersby stare at him, it's early morning. Around eight o'clock, he finally reaches home, dazed with exhaustion, clusters of beards on the sidewalks, standing against the walls.

Wahiba, Méziani's girl, a beautiful perfumed apparition. Moussa hides behind a garbage bin. Waits for her to turn the corner at the end of the street.

Her scent lingers, then evaporates, overpowered by the stench of the garbage.

Moussa comes out of his hiding place, unsteady on his

feet, and heads for the entrance to his building. He trips and lands in a puddle at the feet of a bunch of beards.

Seeing him stumble, Spartacus runs over.

With an abrupt grunt, Moussa tells him to fuck off and leave him alone. The kids gather around, entertainment guaranteed.

Groaning, Moussa gets to his feet, turns to them, and shows them his balls, laughing manically.

Two

A few months later, February, and Moussa's going down-hill fast. Every night, *zombretto*, 6.15, dope. He often laughs hysterically all by himself, behind the garbage bins.

Gazing out to sea, the bay all lit up, he twists a heart out of wire and flings it from the top of the rubbish tip.

Around him, feral kids with glinting eyes play in the refuse.

Each night, before going to sleep, Moussa Massy weeps over his life, huddled against his bit of wall.

Effort down to the barest minimum, he doesn't bother shaving anymore, lets a beard grow. He wears only jog-ging pants and flip-flops, and spends his days propping up the walls of the building with the others.

Topics of conversation: FIS, drugs, black market, bitch women, cocksucking government, emigration. The days drag by, each as boring and hopeless as the last, deliberately ripping the satin skin of dreams.

But every day, more people are getting out. Exodus. Run for your life!

Even Baiza's left. A few months ago, he ditched the

FIS and the kamis. Apparently he's in Amsterdam, working in a pizzeria. He sent photos—he's shaven his beard off and he's wearing a chef's hat.

Djelloul's preparing his application to emigrate to Canada. He begs Moussa to get up off his ass and do the same. But Moussa hasn't the strength, his brain's made of lead.

Djelloul's convinced that Moussa's bewitched, that someone's put the evil eye on him. It's so out of character, this apathy, this defeatism. He even offered to take him to see a healer in Colomb Béchar once, a very good *talib,* to drive out the Devil.

To be honest, Moussa prefers to open another bottle of ethanol.

A new life ruled as straight as a music sheet: get out of bed around ten, outside in flip-flops to lounge against the wall and watch the world go by.

The wall's the perfect observation post, you know all the local goings-on. So-and-so went out with a big bag, his brother-in-law's just come home, someone else has a problem with his starter motor, his neighbor's gone to get some medicine for her daughter, his brother-in-law's just gone out, so-and-so's come back without the big bag.

The wall's also the local totem pole: *Long live the FIS, Down with the FLN, I love Sassia, Allah, Long live Mouloudia, Death to the Kabyles, Long live Abasse Madani, Barcelona mi amor.*

Mohand still hasn't found an apartment. Summer's coming, and this time the wedding will have to go ahead.

So he really is going to bring his wife to live with them. Now they'll be fifteen in the three rooms. They'll be married, so they'll have their own bedroom, but how?

Sniggering, Moussa soon solves the problem by downing two 6.15 tabs. Then he goes and joins the guys in a burnt-out old Renault 5.

Spartacus, Dahmane, and Nordine the sailor. Sandwiches oozing *harissa*, washed down with whiskey. They're not bored. Hi, guys. Moussa half perches on the hood and bites into a *harissa* sandwich followed by a slug of whiskey. Wow . . . body's on fire.

Nordine, who's an ocean-going sailor, brought the whiskey, cheese, and marijuana. Bombay, Djakarta, New York . . . he describes his life at sea, trade, women, adventure. Spartacus's eyes sparkle with gold, his jaw drops in awe as he swallows the yarns the sailor spins.

One day, a postcard arrives from Rachid in Paris urging Moussa to get off his ass and emigrate. He's got to put together a visa application. Once he's in Paris they'll sort things out.

Moussa tosses the card at the kid bin on his way to meet Spartacus at the wall.

Things can always be worse. Look at poor old Spartacus for instance: they're ten to a room, yeah, one room. Almost illiterate, born unemployed. Never had a chance, nothing. He's an insignificant scrap, an offcut, a dropping from Heaven.

Yet he's full of life . . .

◆

One day, Moussa has a household chore to do, got to go fetch a bag of cement from the Parade Ground to fix up the vegetable garden. The builder's arriving at two. Mohand's paid for the cement in advance, given Moussa the receipt, all he has to do is go collect it.

Moussa has trouble waking up. He's on his feet at eight o'clock, it's the crack of dawn for him. To make things worse, Djelloul's not free. Moussa waits at the taxi stand, yawning. A pickup truck suddenly honks at him and Moussa sees Spartacus waving. He's in the back with a sheep, the driver's a buddy.

They have to take the sheep to the Belcourt mosque and slaughter it to feed the poor. Moussa clambers into the pickup truck. The sheep won't stop bleating. They drop Moussa off at the Parade Ground.

At the warehouse, he finds a dense crowd of people waiting in line.

Clutching his receipt, he joins the end of the line, another wagon hitched to the train. The smell of cement, breeze block, plaster, building materials. This is scarce, that's scarce, shortages. Sometimes, there are deliveries— the state—then they allocate them sparingly. Monopoly. Except, of course, if you've got connections, the downstairs neighbor's cousin, apparently he . . .

A decade later, Moussa reaches the desk, holds out his receipt:

Curly auburn-haired clerk:

"Not valid here, you have to go to the Côte Rouge warehouse in Léveilley."

Moussa:

"But . . ."

Curly auburn-haired clerk gets annoyed:

"Move along, next!"

Moussa finds himself outside. Sonofabitch, have to go all the way to Côte Rouge.

Taxi, traffic jams, Moussa reaches the Côte Rouge warehouse. Same routine: long line, Moussa joins the end. Somehow or other he reaches the desk, receipt's valid, phew, he'll get his bag of cement. Heeeave . . . an elderly clerk helps him hoist it over his shoulder. It weighs more than forty-five pounds.

Bent under his load, Moussa leaves and stands by the roadside trying to flag down a cab. Nothing doing, they won't stop, the bastards. What's more, the bag's leaking, there's a hole in the side.

A taxi pulls up, the driver:

"Where to, brother?"

Moussa:

"Cité Mer et Soleil."

"Mmm, not going that way, but I can drop you at the Parade Ground."

Moussa accepts, no choice. They lay down the law, the bastards. He wedges the sack of cement in the trunk of the car.

Moussa checks out the driver. Nasty-looking character. They reach the Parade Ground, that's 80 dinars. Moussa gives him a 200-dinar note and goes to take his sack out of the trunk while the driver rummages for change.

As soon as the sack's out, the car roars off, with his change. Moussa's livid, looks a right moron with the sack of cement between his legs. The sonofabitch really took him for a ride. Country full of motherfuckers: you can't build a nation with this scum, that's for sure.

A guy's crossing the street and heading toward him with a big grin on his face. Long, silky hair . . . seen him somewhere before . . . But can it be him? The young guitarist? American-looking, sang sweet songs in English, at the FLN youth club . . . Shit, that was a long time ago, more than ten years. Effusive greetings, haven't seen you around in ages.

Qays, the guitarist, good-looking kid, classy. Moussa in flip-flops, beard, missing a tooth, sack of cement at his feet.

They chat by the bus stop. Qays:

"I was in the United States, spent eight years over there, but you know, after a while you say to yourself . . . something's missing, smells, know what I mean? Home. So I chucked it all in. I said to myself, come on, go back to your own country, that's where they need you. So here I am. Got back two days ago. So, where's it all going down these days . . . who's playing where? Any good gigs?"

Moussa stares at him and gives a cutting laugh, like a blunt razor blade. Then he heaves his sack of cement onto his shoulder and walks off without a word, leaving Qays at a loss, just standing there.

Moussa's days are regular slaps in the face, barbed smiles, ass propped up against the wall with the others, solidarity in numbers, the primal horde.

Moussa's started playing soccer again with the guys

from the neighborhood, like the good old days when he played for NAHD's under-seventeens. Away matches, singing their hearts out on the coach, the club anthem, fans, blue-and-white flags.

Vital match today: Cité Mer et Soleil against Cité Climat de France. They call it "Climat de Sous-France"– climate of sub-France.

The match is being played on the waste ground. Goalposts: two garbage bins whitewashed and turned upside down. Derdiche is the ref, he's come from Belcourt specially for the occasion. Spartacus is goalie and Moussa's center forward.

The stakes: two big crates of lemon soda, for the spectators, mostly kids. Dahmane's the bookie, taking bets from the crowd. It's a tough one: Mer et Soleil v. Climat de France. Come on, come on, place your bets.

Nobody's got uniforms, of course. Moussa's in an undershirt, ripped jeans, fake Adidas on his feet, no socks; you can feel the shot better.

Spartacus, the goalkeeper, is wearing a kamis. Maybe that's all he's got to wear, poor bastard. How much can one of those things cost?

After forty-five minutes, Mer et Soleil leads six to four, two goals scored by Moussa.

A long pass from Dahmane, Moussa stops it with his chest and dribbles the ball along the touchline. He's flying. One, two, three players and he's alone, facing the opponents' goal. The Mer et Soleil fans are on their feet, going wild. The clamor lends Moussa wings as he prepares to shoot a killer goal from the right.

Suddenly, from the left, the opponents' center back brings him down with a savage kick.

Writhing in pain, Moussa gets up and limps after the center back, egged on by the spectators. He chases him mercilessly the length of the stadium, then hurls himself at him and tackles him just by the rubbish tip.

After giving him a battering with his fists, Moussa shoves his face into a slimy puddle.

✦

Two months later, Djelloul hears that his application to emigrate to Montreal's been accepted. He gives Moussa a brochure, Air Canada, a Canadian couple beside a lake, russet forest. Wordlessly, Moussa crumples the prospectus into a ball and swallows it, as Djelloul looks on, stupefied. Then he bursts out laughing hysterically, in the middle of the street. Everyone looks around.

✦

One day, Moussa's hanging around in Algiers, doing nothing, gray beard, flip-flops. How filthy the place is, garbage collectors' strike, even in the city center, garbage bins open and overflowing, flies, kids. Rue Didouche, country bumpkins everywhere, half-peasant, half-nothing, shortages, endless lines for just about everything.

Concomitant sale: you want a giant Chinese thermos imported by the state? First line up with your brothers, over there. I only want to see one face, get it? That's for the voucher. Then you join the other line, the one over there, the long one, that's it, and once you get to the window, you can finally have your giant Chinese thermos.

But, but, but, but, but, but.

You're forced to buy a pair of underwater goggles, too, old state stock, got to get rid of it . . .

Flick-knife glances, nervous stares, hearts raw. Rue Victor-Hugo. Moussa hesitates: up the hill, rue Debussy?

Victor Hugo, Debussy . . . the names chime like medals, old gold, sleeping legends of an Algiers that certainly once was.

Finally he goes down toward rue Victor-Hugo now overrun by packs of kids dealing in everything under the sun.

Bet they've never heard of Victor Hugo . . .

A whole people rises up and begs for food
Famine in Oran, famine in Algiers
This is what glorious France has done to us!
They say. No maize, no bread. Only grass to graze
And the Arab becomes terrifying and crazed.

Cops buy cigarettes from the kids, black market, got to survive somehow, oh yes, honest family men probably, same hardship, squaring of a very vicious circle. You try sorting out this mess!

Someone calls Moussa's name, he turns around. It's Rabah, the quicksilver guitarist from La Chésa.

Rabah suggests a coffee and stares at Moussa: gap-toothed, straggly beard, ripped jeans, flip-flops. He's the shadow of the ghost of himself.

"What the hell's happened to you? That beard . . . you haven't gone over to the other side, I hope?"

Forced smile, Moussa knows that Rabah must think him a worm:

"No . . . a few small problems . . . and you? Is your band still doing OK?"

"Yeah, we're in Morocco, you know? We're gigging in Agadir. It's fantastic. You ever been to Agadir?"

"No, I've heard about it."

"You'd love it . . . it's paradise. I'm here for a few days to take care of some business, and then I'm off again. Oh, Morocco—the hotels, the clubs, the sea, it's like Acapulco. And best of all, no Islamism over there. The king's put the screws on them. No shortages, no lines, you can get anything you want there. I've taken my wife and my two kids out and it's ciao Algeria. You should come. Everyone's getting out of here. Now's the time, Moussa, before the shit really hits the fan."

Moussa gazes at a fly swimming in his coffee. With his ring finger, he simply fishes it out and flicks it on the ground. Simply.

Then he takes a large slurp:

"You're right, I'm thinking about it. I've got plans."

Good guy, Rabah, they talk about the good old days, La Chésa, anecdotes . . .

Before they part, Rabah gives him his address in Agadir. Moussa writes it down on his cigarette packet and they leave the café.

In the street, they embrace, ciao, see you soon. Rabah

heads off up rue Didouche. Now Moussa has no idea where to go. He wanders where his flip-flops take him.

Empty his mind. He banishes everything from his memory. No more room, got to keep a tight ship. He walks down the sloping rue Meissonnier—this district's a bit like Italy, cool narrow streets, begonias, geraniums on the balconies. Before, it must have been . . .

Oh look, cassette store on the right, check out the window. Hundreds of cassettes displayed in the glare of the sun: rai, Algerian pop, latest disco hits, even the Koran.

In the left-hand corner, Moussa notices his cassette on sale: "MASSY, the new Takfarinas," a real piece of shit.

Smash the window in with his head? Screw his mother?

Whose?

See Lahbib about the rest of the dough?

Wearily, Moussa lets it go. But that's definitely how it starts, when you get *tired*.

Sighing, he lights a cigarette, the last, and crumples the packet with Rabah's address on it.

Moussa throws the packet up in the air, vertically, and juggles it on his left foot, three, four, seven, twelve. Kids come running and count with him, twenty-five, twenty-six, thirty-four, fifty-eight. Finally, after seventy kicks, Moussa sends it flying, a sharp volley with his right foot, and it lands in the empty shopping basket of a poor old woman who hasn't seen a thing.

The kids cheer. Smiling, Moussa buys them a packet

of cigarettes. No Marlboros, so he buys Chélia instead. Taste like straw, but you've got to smoke something.

Relaxed, he makes his way downtown, taking little shady flights of steps with creeping ivy on the walls. He reaches rue Hassiba Ben Bouali.

A silhouette's climbing the steps, a woman. Moussa's heart stops dead.

Is it Fatiha?

Yes, it's her, wearing the hijab. She's pregnant.

Her eyes riveted to the ground, she carries on up the steps, pretending she hasn't seen him.

Sharp daggers pierce the soft vellum of Moussa's soul.

Oh really? Right!

It's nothing. Back home, three bottles of wine, no really, nothing, forget it. A whole packet of 6.15s, and it's sorted. The daggers are gone. Behind the garbage bins facing the sea, with the guys from the neighborhood. Real guys with big hearts.

They're on the wasteland, sitting around a huge, orange fire made of a heap of old tires, like a primitive happening, long flames licking their faces like cats. Dahmane's brought kebabs to grill over the flames, *zombretto,* and hash. Moussa ends up dancing on the moon, his arms outstretched among the stars.

Around 3 a.m., he crawls up to the fifth floor, opens the door to his apartment, and flips his lid.

Completely.

Screaming, he rips his poster into a thousand shreds,

then picks up his mandola and smashes it against the wall, splintering it with every ounce of his strength.

Everyone wakes up and comes running to try and calm him down. Sahnoun's awake too, sitting up on his mattress, his eyes somewhere else. In dressing gowns and nighties, his sisters, Grandma, the whole family pours into the room and tries to stop Moussa.

Ma's feeling poorly, her diabetes, her blood pressure. Ouardia, quick, a glass of water and her pills.

In the bedroom, it's still going on, Moussa's howling his head off. Kicking and punching, he smashes everything he can lay his hands on.

Tripping over Maya and Fella, Mohand tries to tackle him around the waist, Slimane's run off, terrified.

In the corridor, he pushes past Pa who's just woken up. What's all this racket?

Pa stands in the bedroom doorway and stares at the scene, a look of disgust on his face.

With a thrust of the hips, Moussa frees himself from Mohand's grip, and begins to scream even louder, hurling everything on his shelf over the balcony—books, magazines, mementos. Volume 2 of *War and Peace* lands on Spartacus who's hanging around outside.

The crisis is over at daybreak. Moussa silently sobbing in the arms of his grandma who hums a soft Kabyle lullaby. There, there, it's over, it's nothing, it's all right, little one.

◆

Two weeks later, Djelloul's looking for Moussa all over. He finally turns up near Bouhar the baker's. Moussa's tinkering with a car, helping a neighbor take his carburetor apart, two small cups of coffee on the sidewalk.

At the sound of Djelloul's voice, Moussa looks up from the engine and walks over to him, hands black with grease.

Close-shaven, Djelloul's all dressed up. At the corner of the street, a cab's waiting for him, its engine running.

Djelloul can't find the right words: got to split, today, 5 p.m., the airport, Montreal.

He implores Moussa. Wake up, open your eyes, goddammit. You've got to get the hell out, get a visa.

Moussa's glassy eyes stare right through him. They part. Devastated, Djelloul climbs into the cab and leaves.

His face in his grimy hands, Moussa weeps in the street in front of the brats, the Islamists. He aims a violent kick at the coffee cups.

The neighbor comes running, a screwdriver in his hand, what's going on, is there a problem? Has someone died?

Moussa grows more and more irritable, the slightest thing sets him off. Since his violent outburst, no one dares argue with him at home. He slinks in and he slinks out.

One day, Saliha complains about a teacher at school who wants to force her to wear the hijab. He even threatened her once, gave her an ultimatum, just before Eid.

Countless complaints to the head, but no action; three-quarters of the teachers are Islamists.

Cracking his fingers, Moussa tells her he'll wait for her outside school, sort it out, don't worry. Good timing, haven't had much exercise lately.

The next day, he goes to Kouba and waits for Saliha outside the school. Five o'clock, the students pour out, most of them wearing hijabs or kamis. Saliha comes over to Moussa on the sidewalk opposite, and points out the teacher in question.

Very tall, with a black beard and stern gaze, the teacher's chatting to some colleagues. Moussa goes up to him and takes him aside:

"Good evening, sir, I'm sorry to trouble you, I am Miss Boudjiri's brother. I understand there's a . . . problem?"

The teacher's face breaks into a hypocritical smile:

"Problem?"

Moussa acts dumb:

"Yes, something about a hijab, I believe."

Syrupy, the teacher:

"Oh yes! No, it's just a little word of advice. The hijab will protect her from the evil eye. For, as our prophet says, prayers and salvation be upon him, 'When the mouth is closed, the fly cannot enter.'"

Moussa tries to be pleasant, a modern-day feat:

"But why force her if she doesn't want to wear the hijab, 'no religious constraints,' right?"

The teacher tries to explain:

"Yes, no, it's true. But she has to wear the hijab. It's the uniform of purity, the dress of Islam, for . . ."

Completely blinkered, doped up to the eyeballs with the Muslim dream—the prophet's companions, the angels,

Santa Claus. Moussa can't take any more, impossible to talk to him. Change tactics. He thrusts his face close to the teacher's and stops him mid-sentence:

"Right, now you listen to me: she'll never wear the hijab. You leave her alone or I'll screw your mother, understood?"

Stunned, the teacher:

"Excuse me?"

Rush hour, parents coming to pick up their kids, teachers, students, hubbub. The teacher puts down his briefcase and goes for Moussa. Too late, Moussa dodges him, grabs him by the shoulders, and head-butts him twice, hard.

They fight. Moussa sends the teacher flying through the air and pins him to the ground, his knees on the teacher's shoulders. He forces his mouth open and spits into it several times, punching him all the while.

People try to separate them, Islamists rushing to the rescue, kamis to the wind. Moussa leaps up to confront them.

He whips out a long blade, the flick-knife he'd bought in the days of La Chésa.

At the sight of the knife, there's general panic. Students and onlookers scream. Even Saliha begs him to stop. A big circle forms around him.

Moussa cuts his arm and, with his finger, tattoos his face with the blood. Brandishing the blade, he keeps it pointing at the crowd, licking the blood on his finger:

"Come on, you faggots, we're all going to die here.

Let anyone who's not afraid of blood come and get it. I'm a psycho, I warn you. If one of you makes a move, I'll cut your mother open. And if anyone dares bug my sister . . ."

Sorted.

◆

Moussa was born on the first of April—one of nature's jokes, Rachid used to say.

Moussa celebrated his thirty-seventh birthday a few days ago. Sober really, just two bottles of *zombretto* and a few spliffs. Quiet, just him and Spartacus, in silence.

Moussa hardly talks these days, he merely grunts or utters monosyllables, as brief as possible. The essential and basta.

Singing, it's been an age, no longer on the agenda. Except for pissing around with the guys, off his head, banging on the garbage bins, but that's it.

In the pocket of his old ripped-at-the-knees jeans, he finds the FIS sticker he'd confiscated from Slimane. Balled up deep in his pocket, difficult to get it out. Ah! Here it is. Funny how things cling to life.

He smoothes it out, looks at it, not a bad job, professional, then gives it to Spartacus who sticks it on his kamis, thrilled to bits.

◆

Bleak, the following weeks: fundamentalist attacks, disturbances. On 27 May, FIS demo, more than 300,000 people. There's open talk of civil war now, coup d'état, end of the world, earthquake.

Last year's earthquake: racing down the five flights of stairs, the building shudders. Screams, women, kids. As they reached the third floor, violent tremor, Moussa, carrying Maya, fell on top of Slimane. The whole neighborhood out in the street, in their pajamas, underwear, and bathrobes, trembling with fear.

That's when the FIS swelled its numbers, fear of death, huh—cowards! God's punishment, "Fear the Lord, you infidels . . ."

Tensions are running high, Moussa feels like a grenade with its pin pulled out.

Walls, garbage bins, guys, cement-gray days.

Today's news-in-brief: three local guys, including a cousin of Dahmane's, got into a fight over an alternator belt. One dead, two wounded.

Advertising jingles from foreign TV stations blare out from the balconies.

Moussa broods over his dull days, scratching his bushy beard. In front of him, kids fight over his little Elvis Presley mirror, which he's just chucked in a garbage bin.

Moussa hangs around Bouhar's, maybe he'll bump into Spartacus, someone, something to do, anything, before evening. *Zombretto* and 6.15 at the back of the building, facing the sea.

Spartacus isn't around, there's only Dahmane and two

Islamists. Moussa says hello to them and hovers nearby on the edge of the sidewalk. One of the Islamists is just back from Afghanistan, spent a year there. He's talking about the war against the Communist dogs, bivouacking at night, feeling God's immense breath caressing the brows of the faithful, the miracles, when the mujahedin's injuries smelled of musk.

Standing slightly aloof, Moussa's half listening when Spartacus appears. Moussa grabs him, go for walk, roll a joint in the burnt-out Renault 5. Spartacus has just come back from his Islamist brother-in-law who lives in Bainem. All night, he'd been helping him pry the tiles off the floor of his apartment. In the days of the prophet, salvation be upon him, there weren't any tiled floors.

Moussa never answered Rachid's letters. When he phoned, he always told the others to say he wasn't there.

But that day, he got caught out. He'd gone to buy bread from Bouhar's, seven large loaves and six French sticks, same every day, yeah well, fourteen people go through a lot of bread.

As he walks through the door with the basket, the phone rings. Moussa answers. Too late, it's Rachid.

For ten minutes, Rachid bends his ear, yells at him. Get up off your ass and fast, goddammit, fill in the application forms, visa, once you're here, we'll sort it all out.

Moussa hangs up feeling weird. Rachid's voice, it's been a long time, it reminds me . . .

A flurry of memories, silky sensations, green glimmer at the end of the filthy dark tunnel.

Rachid's call seems to have had some effect.

The following days, Moussa focuses, keeps his ears open, picks up info, visa formalities, French Consulate. Not hard, sole topic of conversation.

One day, he decides to wander over there, just to look. The French Consulate.

Three

The French Consulate's near the Place des Martyrs, just behind the huge Treasury Department building.

Moussa, been dreaming all night—the Champs-Élysées, oysters and white wine, Montmartre . . .

It's been a long time since he dreamed about anything.

Moussa's never left Algeria, not even for a day, not even for a vacation. He's amazed by that, too.

Why? Laziness maybe, the hassle, passport, currency . . . and besides, Moussa hates begging and bootlicking, no, that's just not his style.

But now, today, this is it. His mind's made up. He's got the old spark back. The old gold star wants to shine again. The star of Algiers truly wants to fight back, get the hell out, quickly, before . . .

Beautiful sunshine. Whistling, he walks along the seafront and comes out in front of the Consulate.

At least two thousand people standing in line, bunched together, meat for mass consumption, canned meat, William Saurin . . .

He strolls the length of the line, crosses the avenue,

and stations himself in the café opposite. A tea. Ask the waiter, he's bound to have some tips on how to go about things. Moussa offers him a Marlboro.

The waiter takes the cigarette:

"To get a visa, you need proof of residence from someone with the same surname in France. A return plane ticket. Six thousand French francs, that's fifty thousand dinars. Proof of employment—if you're unemployed it's not even . . . A vacation slip. And . . . you have to wait in line. You see that crowd? They've been there since dawn. It's up to you, brother."

No chance, Moussa and red tape just don't get on.

Moussa goes back home, despondent, his dreams at half-mast.

He doesn't touch the spicy stuffed sardines Z'hor's cooked for him, which normally he loves.

Not even anything on TV. Kahina's called him twice to come and watch *Inspector Columbo*.

He goes to bed with a tattered old copy of *Paris-Match*. Mohand comes in for a chat. Is something up?

In the bedroom, Slimane's repairing his little transistor that splutters, Sahnoun's lost in his SAS, and Maya and Fella are tearing up an exercise book, giggling.

Speaking in hushed tones, Moussa tells Mohand everything. Got to get the hell out, visa, forms. Mohand's due to be married in August, he's thrilled someone's freeing up some space:

"Don't worry, I'll help you, Méziane. I know someone

at work who can get you all the documents you need. A real artist. Don't worry, I'll deal with it."

A few days later, Mohand plonks a complete file on Moussa's bed, with his name on it, accurate down to the last detail. It's all forged, but no one would guess—a work of art.

Just need the dough. Moussa scrapes together his savings, asks Grandma, and manages to get together 6,000 French francs for 50,000 dinars, special rate.

The Algiers-Paris return flight, 8,000 dinars. Don't even think about it. Moussa briefly goes back to his bad old ways and dabbles in the black market. Swaps some Marlboros with Spartacus, ten cartons, and there's your ticket.

A hint of spring in his soul, Moussa storms the French Consulate at 5 a.m. He fights tooth and nail to secure a place. To his right, the lacquer sea reflects the sun. It can blind you if you stare at it too long.

Moussa: Arabic for Moses. Rachid told him that. Oh, to part the waves like Moses and walk straight across to La Canebière. Pastis for me!

Around eight o'clock, the line's tripled in length, the crowd, a jittery mass, suddenly surges forward: the offices are opening.

By ten o'clock, it's mayhem. An entire population packed tight, visa meat, stench of sweat. From on high, the sun bakes the backs of necks. Blood boils.

Kids wander up and down selling cigarettes, sandwiches, and warm sodas to the people standing in line.

The crowd inches forward, a grumbling mass of re-
sentment, at the optimistic estimate of five people every
ten minutes, and there are more than two thousand
people here.

Sometimes, people bypass the line and disappear
through the little VIP entrance; friends in high places.
The crowd jeers, the cops give them a thrashing.

Trembling with frustration, Moussa battles his way
through, clenching his buttocks. He holds on, his file
pressed to his chest, moving forward.

The thought of Rachid, Paris, a well-stocked fridge,
sausage and Heineken spurs him on. Real life does exist,
yeah, at the end of the line, can you see it?

The dense throng advances, blind, grilled by the sky.
Moussa's nose is buried in the neck of a tall, frizzy-
haired guy in front of him. Smells like a cowshed. An
old man feels unwell, he's escorted out of the line, glass
of water, people fan him. Moussa shuffles forward,
gains ground.

Around eleven o'clock, he's propelled into the hall.
The counters, whew. Easy little crowd inside, not so hot,
breathe a little.

Outside, the din, the peasants, the infernal sun, the
cops' batons.

Moussa wipes his brow, shirt soaked, sticks to his
skin. Disoriented, what now? He's told to fill in a form,
over there at the desk.

A form. He takes one, gets back some dignity. The

form bears the letterhead: "*République française.*" Wow, this is something else already. It smells good, it's clean.

He fills in the form, copying the information from his file. Then, after standing in line briefly, he's back at the window. Blonde female clerk, Rhône-valley accent, ham-and-wine cheeks.

Beaming, Moussa hands her his greasy file, a huge toothless grin.

With a detached air, she flicks through it, then:

"The vacation slip's missing, sorry. Next . . ."

At a loss, Moussa:

"But . . ."

Cops, he's outside in no time, the seething throng.

Really?

So he goes back home, *zombretto* with the boys, a 6.15, the black sea in front of him. This time he tries something new, it's called Devil's Powder. You crush ten 6.15 tabs and pour the powder into a bottle of *zombretto*.

After shaking the mixture hard, Moussa downs the lot in one go, pure soul-rot. Spartacus suggests he puts the brakes on, ease up a little. But Moussa doesn't give a fuck. He repeats the mix three times, with a few joints to spice it up.

Seriously wasted, he's never been so out of it.

Around 4 a.m., people come and wake Mohand. It's Moussa.

Fifth-floor landing, doors gaping, neighbors in pajamas, bathrobes, whispering, rumors . . . Moussa . . . waste ground . . . odd. Maybe something's wrong.

In jogging pants and slippers, Mohand goes down to

get Moussa, holding a flashlight. He finds him in a coma, lying on the waste ground near the garbage bins.

Parnet Hospital, emergency ward, race there in Saliha's Ritmo.

In the lobby, hot as a steam bath, a/c broken, condenser blown, ordered a replacement six months ago.

Duty doctor absent, ditto his assistant, the orderly's in charge. War veteran, hairy chest naked to the wind, he sips a tea and chats with patients sitting on the floor.

Cockroaches cross the lobby and crawl into the big medicine fridge that hasn't worked in three months.

In one corner, the Islamist patients. Prayer by the washrooms with the doors gaping.

Mohand starts to shout.

"My brother's about to die, for fuck's sake, someone get a stretcher!"

The sullen orderly ambles over, flicking his cigarette ash onto the ground:

"There aren't any, brother. We've got three but they're all being used, look. We ordered new ones ages ago."

Mohand sees three injured patients lying on stretchers in the lobby, open wounds, dirt, puddles on the floor.

Mohand gesticulates and yells louder, threatening to complain to the authorities.

Male nurse in stained white coat comes up, chewing tobacco, transistor radio in his pocket, Iglésias:

"What's going on here? Keep the noise down."

Mohand explains, his brother Moussa, coma, in the car,

stretcher. The nurse, crushing two cockroaches at once with his left flip-flop:

"All right, calm down, we'll have a look. Are you parked far?"

"No, just there."

They go out and bring Moussa, still lifeless, into the main ward.

A guy with multiple stab wounds lurches in, escorted by three gendarmes. The man's ear has been sliced off, it's hanging by a ribbon of flesh. Blood everywhere. Two nurses rush over, stitch him up right there, in the chair.

Another emergency bursts in, with the cops this time, two wounded, car crash, arm torn off, ribs smashed.

Everyone's bawling, arms raised, sorry, X-ray department out of action, no Band-Aids, gauze, ether, even our scissors have been stolen.

Mohand and the nurse lay Moussa across two chairs, waiting room strewn with the injured, the walking wounded amble around.

Local layabouts are here, too. Bored, can't sleep in this heat. In undershirts and flip-flops, playing dominos with the orderly, staff, and patients.

Mohand goes to the washroom for some water. Blocked squat toilet inundated with urine, turds, right up to the door. Impossible to set foot inside.

Washbasin. Holding his nose, Mohand turns on the faucet. Nothing. Water's cut off.

A patient who's just managed a long-range piss hands him a bowl with a dribble of water in it. Mohand takes the bowl and has a quick sip, closing his eyes.

Cigarette dangling from his lip, the nurse examines Moussa's eyes, his pupils. The ash from his cigarette drops onto his white coat. He vaguely brushes it off:

"Mmm, *zombretto* and 6.15. Classic, we get these every day. Sometimes just kids, completely fucked. But don't worry, I'll give him an injection, and after a good sleep, he'll be fine. But he can't carry on like this, you have to talk to him. Has he got . . . problems?"

Mohand, stunned:

"Problems? I . . ."

The nurse prepares the syringe in a rusty tray, spits out his tobacco, and gives Moussa the injection without disinfecting the skin. Nothing before. Or after.

◆

Twelve hours later, Moussa opens his eyes, the whole family's around his bed, except Pa.

His sisters have made him egg pancakes, Grandma's stroking his forehead, muttering to herself.

Once they're alone together, Moussa tells Mohand the whole story: visa refused, vacation slip, sick of life, can't take any more. Mohand comforts him, laughing, don't worry, tomorrow you'll have your vacation slip, forget about it.

Big brother's word. Next day, around 7 p.m., Mohand places the form on the kitchen table.

French Consulate, two days later, and Moussa's back on the attack. At 5 a.m. sharp, he's already in the crowd. He knows the score. Here we go, cheek to cheek, skin to skin, breath rank with oil and dread. Moussa grits his teeth, carried along by the vast body of the crowd.

Eleven-fifteen: at last he's standing at the counter. He hands over his file to the blonde clerk with ham-and-wine cheeks:

". . . I'm sorry, there's a new law. We need a telex confirming your hotel reservation in Paris. Next . . ."

Moussa finds himself on the sidewalk alone with his rage. Behind him, whoops of joy, applause.

He turns back. People are crowding around someone who's just been given his visa. That's the way it is, the minute someone gets one, everyone wants to see the visa with their own eyes, stroke it, kiss it. You never know, it might bring luck.

Curiosity pushes Moussa toward the lucky man.

Surrounded by some thirty gaping onlookers, the blessed man seems to have a special aura. Moussa can hardly make out his face. Could it be Réda? The good-looker, taxi driver, Stevie Wonder? Yes, it's him.

Moussa doesn't dare go up to him. He skulks past and disappears. The visa passes from one hand to another.

Stricken, he goes home, sticks his ass to the wall along with Spartacus, Dahmane, and others, and others, and others and others.

New wall-props, young relief crew. They don't know their own minds anymore, one day they're Islamists, the next *zombretto,* often both: *zombretto*-Islamism.

Moussa gives Spartacus 100 dinars. Score anything—dope, 6.15s, see things clearer. Spartacus comes back with some 6.15s, perfect. Dahmane suggests going behind the building, the waste ground, the garbage bins, the sea with its soft swell.

Dahmane produces a stick of hash, rolls a giant spliff, a four-skinner, and invites Moussa to light it after he's dedicated it to God.

Yes . . . this is God, a joint that's passed and passed back from one person to another . . .

Strange how mild the weather is, silky, sun setting, birds of the twilight hour in the distance.

Moussa thinks of Sahnoun, autism, no, don't end up like him.

It was in 1972 Sahnoun flipped his lid. The security police had found Berberist leaflets on him. They tortured him, shoved a bottle up his ass. Mohand told me.

Since then, Sahnoun hasn't opened his mouth: an eternal silence.

Calm down, get the fuck out, phone Rachid, he must be able to do that for me, telex a fucking hotel reservation.

Excited now, Moussa leaves the gang around 10 p.m., goes back up to his place, and dials Rachid's number in Paris.

It's the first time he's called him.

As soon as he hears Rachid's voice, tears . . . he can feel Paris in the phone, background music, fridge bursting with sausage and Heineken. Simple simplicity, to live a normal life normally, the simplest, most normal there is, no more.

Rachid promises him the telex at once, no problem, hang in there, we can do this.

The next day, letter from Rachid, the telex, via Sid Ali, flight attendant on the Paris-Algiers route.

These days, Moussa barely sleeps, eats very badly, has a brittle temper.

Monday evening, he picks up his file and sleeps under the stars with everyone else in Place des Martyrs, opposite the Consulate.

Doesn't get a wink all night, flasks of whiskey, 6.15, joint after joint, waiting for 5 a.m.

First glimmer of dawn and he's at the front of the line, praying to Vishnu or whoever for it to go right this time.

Nine o'clock, thick crowd, an oily paste of men. Boys stand in line from dawn for nothing, to sell their place, 500 dinars. Moussa shuffles forward, a millimeter at a time.

At the window, he hands over his file, ham-and-wine cheeks, the blonde clerk:

"Oh I'm sorry, your last three pay slips are missing. Next . . ."

Moussa finds himself out on the sidewalk again, the cops are quick with their batons here.

Gutted, hangdog, he walks home, fucking shit fucking race in this fucking shit fucking country!

The seafront boulevard, brain on fire, all alone, talks to himself out loud, people stare.

The liners, the jetty, the seagulls, Moussa opens his file and scatters the papers from the sea wall. One by one, the vacation slip, certificate of employment, hotel reservation telex. The papers whirl through the air, dead leaves in the sun, and slowly sink down into the murky waters of the docks.

That's it, finished, never talk about it again, not about the visa, or anything. That's it, forget it. Move on to other things, like how to spend this evening?

Inject *zombretto* into his eye, or fuck someone over for real, like Baiza, pow, stab them in the belly?

Yeah, but who?

Whoever . . . the first person to come along.

Level with the main Post Office, Moussa spots a passerby, average executive type, briefcase, tie. He pretends to ask him the time and goes for it. Two massive head butts and he leaves him to soak in his own blood. Moussa quickly disappears down the narrow streets, the walk does him good, finds himself in Belcourt, outside the mosque.

Islamist demo, incense, musk, desiring instant death, weeping. Kids not even three years old leading the procession, wearing kamis, carrying Korans bigger than they are. Right behind, dozens of girls in hijabs demanding strict and immediate application of the *sharia*.

Behind them, the mass of troops, marching, one, two, one, two, one, two, strict segregation, have to sort the wheat from the chaff. Moussa cuts across the demonstration—a gash across a face.

He keeps going, up the hill, the first apartment buildings appear.

On the verge a broken-down car, a lovely, brand-new Peugeot 309. The driver, must be a Frenchman, sixtyish, head under the hood looking bemused.

Moussa, local Mr. Fix-it, goes over:

"Do you have a problem, sir?"

The driver, muttering:

"Yes, um, I don't know what's wrong. It won't start."

Moussa, heart of gold:

"Let's have a look."

He rolls up his sleeves and plunges his hands into the grease, checks everything, tightens the battery-lead connections.

"Now try."

The engine immediately begins to throb:

"Oh, that's marvelous! I don't know how to thank you. Can I give you some money? It's the least . . ."

Moussa, moved: a Frenchman?

"No, no, it's my pleasure."

The Frenchman:

"My name's Courval, I work at the French Consulate. If I can ever do anything for you . . ."

Moussa stops listening, Paris already singing in his ears, the sweet pom-pom melody, breeze on the banks of the Marne, white wine, open-air dances . . .

He pockets Courval's business card, telephone number, address. Then they part.

That evening, it's party time on the wasteland, Moussa and Spartacus, six bottles of wine, just the two of them, dope and 6.15s, too. Paris trips golden among the garbage bins, the air is magical. You can even see the métro quite clearly, the wide avenues, the bars, the blonde Parisian girls . . .

◆

Two days later, Moussa picks up the phone. Courval invites him to his home, so they can discuss things in private. Honored, Moussa shaves for the first time in months, and puts on a clean shirt and jeans.

Courval's magnificent villa outside the city, near Birkhadem, a sensual garden, rosebushes, carnations, jasmine arbor, Moorish patio, soft orange light on the balcony.

A beautiful night, scent of peony and basil. Courval offers Moussa a drink, a well-chilled Kronenbourg.

After a few polite formalities and a second beer, Moussa brings up his worries:

". . . yes, you understand, I can't live here any longer, I have to get to France, I've got friends waiting for me. And . . . I've been refused a visa three times at the Consulate."

Courval, smiling:

"Oh, that can be arranged, I don't think there'll be any difficulty getting you a visa. I can do that. So long as we understand each other."

As he talks, Moussa hears warning bells. What? Oh . . . Weird.

Courval, affable, draws closer, closer.

Warning bells, double weird . . .

Then it clicks. Moussa finally gets it: Courval's gay. The impetuous, beautiful young North African boys, Gide, Genet, Barthes . . .

No, never done it. Not at all his scene. Moussa simultaneously puts down his beer and stands up, politely indignant.

Courval, even more aroused by this rebel Adonis, groans with desire:

"Listen, be nice to me, Moussa, and you'll get a one-year visa. I'll give you names of people for the residence permit. I know quite a few people in the administration in Paris."

Paris, the canaries of Belleville and the merry-go-rounds of Créteil dance before his eyes. A residence permit. Will he or won't he? His dream is there, within his grasp. Visa, the Arc de Triomphe, Boulevard Saint-Michel, lovely cool weather. Moussa drops the formality. His mind's made up, he sits down again:

"Got any whiskey?"

Suave, charming, Courval produces a bottle of JB. Moussa downs more than half of it, in three long slugs straight from the bottle.

Then, with a flourish, he stands up and claps his hands:

"OK, I'm all yours, Courval."

Much later, the muezzin, dawn, Moussa stares at himself in the mirror as he washes his face.

Breakfast, orange juice, honey, jam, coffee, milk. Wearing a silk bathrobe, Courval hands him a letter of recommendation, which he's just written, diaphanous hands, presidential fountain pen.

Moussa avidly skims the letter, recommendation, one-year visa, promises are made to be kept.

He gets back late in the afternoon, elated, looks for

Spartacus. He finds him with a bunch of beards commenting on the events of the night before. Violent clashes between the FIS and the Army, a hundred dead in Place du Premier-Mai, they say. The Army opened fire.

Moussa doesn't give a shit, doesn't want to know, they can all go fuck themselves. He tugs Spartacus's sleeve and proudly shows him Courval's letter.

'Not a word about er . . . you know, the thing with Courval . . ."

Spartacus is thrilled, they have a quick swig of *zombretto* and decide to go and spend the night outside the Consulate, with the great visa hordes, until the office opens in the morning.

Spartacus insists on coming, he's bored and so happy for Moussa.

On the way, they see columns of tanks moving into position at strategic road junctions, jeeps and military trucks around the working-class districts.

Orders, counterorders, soldiers at a run, bayonets cocked, what the hell's going on?

Is this war?

Moussa buys a paper, 5 June 1991: "*State of siege declared, Prime Minister resigns.*" Shit, this really stinks . . .

Tanks surround Place des Martyrs, soldiers, walkie-talkies. Moussa and Spartacus find a spot close to the big kiosk. Not many people, other than the visa veterans preparing to spend the night here, too, be first in line at dawn.

Night falls fast, right opposite, the port, the sea and the great Ketchaoua mosque surrounded by tanks.

The crowd that sleeps here's well organized—emergency solidarity. They pass around cigarettes, joints, food, coffee.

They also pass around rumors, state of emergency, civil war, coup d'état, visa embargo, borders closed.

Moussa, *in extremis,* go through the slender eye of the needle like a thread, quick. Then ciao, pick up his life again, change race, sex, soul, religion, nationality. Israeli even, who cares?

From time to time, soldiers pass among them, armed to the teeth, heavy-handed ID checks, scrutinize the faces, especially the Islamists'. They give Spartacus a hard time because of his kamis, his beard. But as soon as they smell the *zombretto* on his breath, they leave him alone.

Moussa and Spartacus are well equipped, *merguez* sandwiches, 6.15s, joints.

Moussa takes out Courval's letter again, a real delicacy. He savors it for the thousandth time, Courval's flourishing signature, the gilt letterhead "*Consulat de France.*"

Spartacus can't read, strokes the grain of the fine paper admiringly, the contours of the signature.

In spite of the soldiers, Moussa dreams of Paris all night. Magnificent moonlight.

Neither of them has ever set foot in Paris, or ever left Algeria. Fantasies, born of borrowed images, grafted memories, from friends of friends who've told them about it.

Moussa stares into the void. He can see himself in Paris. The moment he arrives, the first thing he'll do is

193

order a ham sandwich with butter and a well-chilled Heineken.

And the second is have a proper, normal bath, like in the ads, and wash, wash, wash, wash.

After that, have to see where things are at. Rachid, his friends. He rubs his hands, he's already in Paris. The taste of that ham sandwich with butter on his lips, on his tongue, yes, he's there.

Spartacus knows he can't even dream of dreaming of getting a visa, leaving or anything. Moussa knows it, too. Spartacus is . . . a whole different problem, poor kid.

Five o'clock, the crowd gradually takes shape, a little bud, Moussa and Spartacus are in front, charge! Rowing in a sea of men, Moussa floats, lets the tide carry him.

Cops in position, crowd denser, sun already beating down.

A lot of regulars, familiar faces, friendly nods.

Around 9 a.m., the crush begins. Spartacus and Moussa stick together, pushing forward, forward.

Then suddenly, it hits him . . .

But I don't need to stand in line, do I? Idiot! I should be able to go straight in, recommendation, the little VIP door.

Checks with his neighbor in the crowd, PhD in visa procedures.

Barely able to contain themselves, they drop out of the line and head toward the little VIP entrance. Spartacus waits for him proudly outside the line. See Moussa's visa, give him a hug.

So Moussa gets priority access. People grumble, whistle,

connections, the bastards. An Islamist yells, waving his fist, insulting Moussa who tries to explain:

"But . . . recommendation."

This fuels the Islamist's fire. He goes up to Moussa:

"And what's more you stink of alcohol! Filthy pork eater!"

That does it. Moussa completely loses it. He goes berserk, grabs the Islamist by the beard, flings his file to the ground. Moussa's in a frenzy, yanking at the Islamist's beard. Spartacus tries to intervene, no way, too late, the machine's out of control, Moussa's become someone else.

Big fight. Moussa won't let go of the Islamist's beard, Paris, bam, bam, Fatiha, smash his head in, bam, music, against the sidewalk, bam, bam, Rachid. Hysterical, Moussa's getting his revenge, bam, Algeria, keeps pounding until the cops and soldiers come and overpower him.

Bad news. Lying face up on the sidewalk, the Islamist is dead.

Epilogue

Moussa was referred to the public prosecutor for first-degree murder and sentenced to twenty-five years' detention. He was sent to El Harrach prison.

He spends the first six months unable to speak to anyone. His day-to-day life is reduced to the misery of jail routine—walks in the prison yard, the mess hall. The rest of his time is spent in a shared cell with more than fifty men on mats.

He grows a long beard, which he strokes constantly. He doesn't answer the letters he receives from Rachid, Djelloul, or anyone else.

One day, walking in the yard, he meets Mustapha, Fatiha's brother, a fundamentalist arrested for political reasons. They soon become inseparable. Fatiha has two kids now.

Mustapha and Moussa see each other every day. Their friendship helps Moussa start taking an interest in things again. He joins the prison soccer team.

Each day, Mustapha talks to him of God and Islam, the only way out in this cowardly, hypocritical world.

Moussa listens to Mustapha closely, asks questions, seeks to understand.

The weeks pass. Moussa manages to get hold of a copy of the Koran and pores over the age-old sacred texts burning with truth and wisdom.

One day, he swaps his clothes for a kamis and starts spending a lot of time with the many faithful at the prison mosque. He joins in all the rites, ablutions, genuflections, and prayers, becoming a regular devotee.

A soft glow gradually illuminates his soul as he reads the sacred text. He willingly submits to the rigorous meter, flamboyant rhetoric, and monumental inspiration of its lyricism.

Within a few months, he has learned the entire Koran by heart. Then he starts reading the great exegeses. He devours dozens of Islamic works as he tries to understand the quarrels between the schools and different sects. He painstakingly analyzes Boukhari, Tabari, Abu El Fida, El Mawdoudi, and attempts to fathom the obscurities of the Sharia, jurisprudence, the four rites of Islam, Hanefite, Malekite, Chafeite, and Hanbalite.

On hearing of President Boudiaf's assassination, Moussa fasts for a week as an offering to God. He is convinced that it's a Sign, the opening of the great blessed way.

His learning makes him something of an authority among the inmates, even those close to the FIS leaders. They treat him with deference, coming to consult him on the finer points, disputes over matters of interpretation. His face the picture of serenity, Moussa always resolves *the matter justly, the sword of truth slicing along the exact boundary between Good and Evil.*

Prison wisdom, the culture of resignation and repentance all intermingle in a fabulous, refined Gongoresque fabric woven from faith and piety, caressed by the munificent hand of God. He also runs into Gabès of Belcourt, the madman. Oh, he's calmed down now, thanks to reading the Book. Gabès becomes Moussa's right-hand man, his secretary and devoted clerk. Gabès is mesmerized by Moussa's saintly appearance as he sits cross-legged, stroking his long gray beard.

Even Mustapha is full of admiration for Moussa's self-denial and awesome spirituality. A sort of invisible light seems to emanate from him. Everybody feels it.

The first intellectuals, writers, and journalists are executed. Tahar Djaout, Laâdi Flici, Boukhobza, Professor Bousebci, and many others end up with their throats slit or with bullets through their heads. The list grows longer each day—women, children, prosecutors, ordinary citizens.

The repression is atrocious. Moussa learns that Spartacus was tortured to death, for nothing.

The Islamist prisoners are in a ferment. This is it, the true Jihad. The faithful flock to Moussa's cell, where Gabès maintains order. He sits the faithful in a circle around Moussa. They have all come to seek Moussa's wise opinion, his interpretation of the situation. There's talk of armed groups, Afghans, the resistance, an excited murmur ripples through the assembled men.

Sitting on his carpet, a string of beads in his hand, Moussa slowly raises his hand above their heads. Absolute silence, they all hang on his every word. In a quavering, reedy voice, Moussa at last delivers his interpretation, preceded by five citations from the Koran.

For him, this is the unmistakable start of Jihad against anyone who dares refute the splendor of the values of Islam. The Last Judgment is nigh, let each person prepare to open and read the book of his life, the reckoning will be just. Death to hypocrites, unbelievers, and Communists. No mercy, eradicate the vermin at the source, eliminate adulterous women and bastard children at will. Uproot the weeds forever, purify the revered shield of Islam, so that His Glory may shine in all four corners of the universe.

With blazing eyes he declares that he approves Iran's renewal of the fatwa against Salman Rushdie, the pork-eating agent of international Zionism and of the West. The sword will purify all, blood must flow for the truth to reign, for such is the will of the Almighty. In raptures, Moussa approves the executions, urges more. For him, it is a crucial act of faith, the basic duty of all honest Muslims.

His audience is enthralled by his magnetism, his luminous charisma. He makes them repeat Allah O Akbar seven times in unison. The prison walls shudder with their cries, many of the prisoners feel their blood run cold.

◆

Moussa is soon adopted by the brotherly network of the enlightened, the immense arm of God, the Absolute

Purity of the Way. His fanaticism brings him to the attention of the jail authorities for political activism. He is transferred to Lambèze, the harshest prison, where they send the psychos, the hard-core criminals.

A forbidding ancient fortress on a remote plain, Lambèze prison is tough on discipline, obedience. Moussa finds this a source of strength, tempers the bronze of his soul in it, seeing the white face of Salvation beyond the veil of the illusory real.

This is where he forges the true, definitive shape of his destiny. Brilliant illuminations entirely dedicated to the Glory of the One, the Only.

On contact with the true leaders of the FIS, heroes of the people, Moussa's exceptional determination proves itself with every passing day. Among the Islamist prison population, he has already become a legend. They call him "Noor"—light—which has been his religious name for quite some time now.

The attacks on intellectuals, artists, and foreigners are becoming more widespread. Mass hysteria rules, the infidels scuttle off like rats to their holes, the government is at a loss; nothing can stop the light.

Noor coordinates operations from Lambèze, selecting the victims—writers, men of culture, lawyers, female elementary schoolteachers. They are decapitated, emasculated, and their throats slit. Erase forever any trace of the deep, thorough crusade led by the French in Algeria.

Noor soon joins the main phalanx, those who decide which way the winds of the Islamist movement will blow.

They value his skills as a political strategist. His analyses are always pertinent, his options radical, his faith clear and unwavering.

He gradually moves farther and farther up the hierarchy until he is appointed emir by the leaders of the Islamist Army, with the blessing and august approval of sheikhs Abassi Madani and Ali Benhadj, also incarcerated for years in a military jail.

Emir Noor is one of the thousands of escapees from Lambèze, liberated by the glorious Islamic Army, forty trucks filled with brothers. He masterminded the breakout and was the inside contact.

Everything went according to plan, a plan honed over several long months.

Bribe the guards won over to the cause, cut the phone lines, let the brothers into the jail, orchestrate the massacre and the great escape in trucks.

That day, before the operation, Emir Noor withdrew into a long, silent prayer. Deep meditation, strict orders not to be disturbed. Gabès was there to send people away.

When the time came, Emir Noor and Gabès slipped silently into the guardroom. Three guards. Allah O Akbar, *the knives slid under their throats. Blood purifies. Next they neutralized all the sentries in the watchtowers, by the knife. Then they flung open the prison gates and the brothers streamed into the mess hall, the entrance, the dormitories. Total carnage, virtually no resistance.*

Just before the attack, Emir Noor and Gabès raced

into the guardroom to get the keys to the cells. The emir was toting a Kalashnikov thrown him by a brother as he ran past. In the guardroom, a dozen soldiers, young conscripts playing cards. In the name of God, the emir turned his Kalashnikov on them and emptied it, aiming at their heads, while Gabès finished off the wounded with his knife.

The infernal shoot-out lasted more than two hours, Kalashnikovs blasting, grenades exploding and destroying as they opened up an escape route.

In a corner, a trembling young conscript on his knees recited the profession of faith. Without batting an eyelid, Gabès stabbed him in the jugular.

Then they unlocked all the cells and a thousand brothers boarded the waiting trucks, which drove off into the nearby mountains, the scrubland. En route, they picked up weapons, ammunition, walkie-talkies, and military vehicles.

Today, Emir Noor is an eminent member of the GIA. He lives in the Djidjel maquis, organizes attacks, slits the victims' throats with his own hand, and curses the West.

Glossary

ALLAH O AKBAR God is great.

BERBER The Berbers lived in North Africa long before the arrival of the Arabs, and their culture probably dates back more than 4,000 years. Today, there are substantial Berber populations in Morocco and Algeria, plus smaller numbers in Tunisia, Libya, and Egypt. Berbers are identified primarily by language, but also but traditional customs and culture—such as the distinctive music and dances.

BURNOUS Hooded cloak

CHAÂBI Popular music descended from the multifarious forms of Moroccan folk music. Originally performed in markets, it is now found at any celebration or meeting.

CHADLI President of Algeria 1979–1992

DERBOUKA Drum made of goatskin stretched over a terracotta base

EID Festival celebrating the end of Ramadan (period of fasting)

205

EMIR	Commander
FFS	Socialist Forces Front
FIS	Front islamique du salut (Islamic Salvation Front) founded in 1989
FLN	Front de libération nationale (National Liberation Front) founded in the late 1950s to fight French colonialism
GANDOURA	Short, loose, sleeveless garment
GIA	Groupe Islamique Armée (Armed Islamic Group)
GONGORESQUE	An affected type of diction and style introduced into Spanish literature in the 16th century by the poet Gongora y Argote (1561–1627)
HARISSA	Hot sauce made from chillies, widely used in North Africa
HIJAB	Veil
IMF	International Monetary Fund
IN SH'ALLLAH	God willing
KABYLE	Kabyle is an Afro-Asiatic language spoken by the Kabyle people. The Kabyle are an African Berber tribe located primarily in Morocco, Tunisia, Western Libya, and the coastal mountain regions of northern Algeria. There are a total of over 3,000,000 speakers in all countries. The majority are in Algeria, where there are 2,500,000 speakers

KAMIS
: Loose shirt, the Afghan dress of the Jihadists (advocates of a Holy War against unbelievers)

KÉPI
: Peaked cap, emblematic of the police

MAGHREB
: A region of northwest Africa comprising the coastlands and the Atlas Mountains of Morocco, Algeria, and Tunisia

MANDOLA
: A member of the mandolin family of instruments. Like a mandolin it has four courses of paired strings. It is a little bigger than a mandolin, giving it a deeper more complex voice.

MAQUIS
: The scrubland where the resistance fighters took refuge. Synonymous with the underground movement.

MERGUEZ
: Spicy sausage

PIED-NOIR
: French colonial born in Algeria

RAI
: Form of folk music, originated in Oran, Algeria, from Bedouin shepherds, mixed with Spanish, French, African-American, and Arabic musical forms, which dates back to the 1930s. Since the late 1970s, a form of pop-oriented rai has become popular throughout the Middle East, North Africa and Europe.

RCD
: *Rassemblement pour la Culture et la Démocratie*—Union for Culture and Democracy), founded in 1989 and directed by Saïd Saidi. RCD is part of the "eradication' movement," which calls for the suppression

of Islamists by force. RCD left the government one week after the onset of the riots
in Kabylia in spring 2001.

SALAM   Peace be upon you (traditional greeting).
  ALAIKOUM

SAS   Special Air Services, a specialist regiment
               of the British Army that is trained in
               commando techniques of warfare and
               used in clandestine operations

SHARIA   Islamic law

TALIB   Teacher

WILLIAM SAURIN Dinty Moore

ZOMBRETTO   A concoction of ethanol and grenadine
               syrup

Key Dates in Recent Algerian History

1830 France invades Algeria.

1879 Northern Algeria is declared part of France. Europeans living in Algeria are given full citizenship, but Algerians can only obtain citizenship if they renounce Islam. While all Algerians are considered French subjects, they are prohibited from holding public meetings, carrying weapons, or moving around the country without permission.

1901 Algeria obtains economic autonomy.

1920s Algerian nationalism grows among sections of the population disappointed at not receiving full equality with the French.

1942 Algeria becomes the seat of de Gaulle's exiled government during World War II.

1947 The founding of the Algerian parliamentary assembly, with equal numbers of Muslims and Europeans. But this institution never receives sufficient support from either side to become effective.

1954   The committee that soon came to be called Front de Libération Nationale (FLN) is set up in Egypt by Algerian exiles. The FLN starts guerrilla and terrorist activities in Algeria, mainly in the countryside. France responds by sending in troops. The FLN's strategy of fomenting fear is soon emulated by the French, and acts of violence are committed by both sides.

1956   The fighting spreads to the cities. The French gain ground.

1958   Heavy pressure is put on the French government from French opposition and French settlers in Algeria to find a solution to the conflict.

   May 2   De Gaulle is asked to form a new government in France, as there is a serious political crisis in the country.

1959   De Gaulle declares that he will allow Algeria to chose between independence or continued association with France.

1960, 1961   Unsuccessful revolts by Army generals against de Gaulle in France.

1961 *January 8*   70 percent of Algerians, and 76 percent of French people vote for geographically restricted independence for Algeria.

1962 *March 18*   The Evian Agreement. The FLN, the French government, and the Algerian government in exile agree that independence is to be given to Algeria after a transitional period, and after referendums in both Algeria and France.

100,000 French and about 1,000,000 Algerians are estimated to have been killed in the 8 years of fighting.

April 8 91 percent vote in favor of Algerian independence. The French nationalists do not accept this and continue to carry out terror attacks.

April 20 The leader of the French nationalists, Raoul Salan, is arrested and deported to France.

July 1 99.7 percent Algerians vote for independence.

July 3 Independence is proclaimed. Mass emigration of Europeans starts, even though their protection and full civil rights are guaranteed. Algeria is left with a serious shortage of skilled labor.

August 3 The FLN and the government in exile join forces and agree to hold elections.

September 28 Ahmed Ben Bella forms the first government of free Algeria.

1965 Minister of Defense Houari Boumedienne stages a coup; Ben Bella is toppled but without bloodshed. Ben Bella's power had for some time been growing at the expense of the National Assembly. Boumedienne takes supreme power for himself. Algeria makes full use of its oil resources, and enters the international arena, as a revolutionary, efficient, and fast-growing developing country.

1976 Algeria is declared a socialist state, under control of the FLN. Boumedienne is elected president.

1978 *December 27* Death of Boumedienne. Benjedid Chadli is elected as the new president. His political style is similar to Boumedienne's, but he exerts less fierce control.

1980 "Spring of Kabyle," a rebellion in Tizi Ouzou and Bejaïa against Arab cultural and political dominance. Nobody is killed, but this incident is very important for Kabyle identity in the face of the Arabization of Algeria.

1988 Riots against government policies in Algiers and some other cities. At least 500 youths are killed in Algiers.

1989 A new constitution allows political parties other than the FLN.

1990 Front Islamique du Salut, the Islamic Salvation Front, (FIS), wins a landslide victory in the provincial and municipal elections.

1992 After the first round of the national elections, where the FIS has a clear win, Chadli is forced to resign by a group of military and civilian officials. Elections are cancelled and a state of emergency is declared. Muhammad Boudiaff is elected new president, but he is assassinated later the same year. After him a five-member group fills the vacancy. Violence breaks out, with the Islamists attacking everyone associated with the government as well as ordinary people acting in what they see as an "immoral" manner, and foreigners from selected countries (countries supporting the government–France is one of the main targets). The government sends military troops and police forces against the Islamists, as well as their supporters.

AZIZ CHOUAKI was born in 1951, grew up in Algeria with his mother, and learned to play the guitar to the music of the Beatles, the Rolling Stones, Jimi Hendrix—music later forbidden by the regime. For political reasons, he has lived in France since 1991, where he has published novels and plays. His most recent novel is *Arobase*.

Since 1980, **ROS SCHWARTZ** has translated numerous fiction and nonfiction titles from the original French, and **LULU NORMAN** specializes in translating North African authors.

The translators wish to thank Olivier Cormier Otaño, Moris Farhi, David Katznelson, Rémi Labrusse, Polly McLean, Daniel Miller, Chloe Schwartz, and Leo Schwartz.

The text of *The Star of Algiers* has been typeset in Rotis, a font designed in 1989 by Otl Aicher for Agfa; his last type design. Book design by Wendy Holdman. Composition by Stanton Publication Services, Inc., St. Paul. Manufactured by Bang Printing on acid-free paper.